I Dreamt I Was in Heaven

The Rampage of The Rufus Buck Gang

Maoma July, Sam Sampson, Rufus Buck, Luckey Davis, Lewis Davis

I Dreamt I Was in Heaven

The Rampage of The Rufus Buck Gang

LEONCE GAITER

LEGBA BOOKS

I Dreamt I Was in Heaven

The Rampage of The Rufus Buck Gang

Published by Legba Books

ISBN-13: 978-0-615-49010-6
ISBN-10: 0-615-49010-7

www.BuckRampage.com
www.LeonceGaiter.com

Printed in U.S.A

For James

"Even strongly-marked differences occasionally appear in the young of the same litter, and in seedlings from the same seed-capsule. At long intervals of time, out of millions of individuals reared in the same country and fed on nearly the same food, deviations of structure so strongly pronounced as to deserve to be called monstrosities arise;"

- Charles Darwin
"The Origin of Species"

I can't go back to Paradise no more.
I killed a man back there.

- Bob Dylan

The crowd murmured. Hushed. Expectation sucked the air right out of it. Torches flickered uselessly; their meager light only showcased the dread. Shadows writhed on the crowd's long, drawn faces. Men, women, Indian, Negro, but mostly white men's faces. Fear and rage skittered across each as if in competition. Rage wanted it all. Each man sought to bathe in revenge for the wrongs done, real and imagined, by those who by dint of color hadn't any right—any right at all. But fear checked it. A fear that each fought to deny to himself, and more importantly, to hide from the man standing next to him,

"I can see 'em!"

Murmurs rose to whispers. The whole crowd shuffled cautiously forward and stopped, as if frightened to move any further. Then silence. Even the murmurs stopped. Above their own breathing they heard the creaking of a laden wagon, the horse hooves clomping on the dry dirt road. Each in the crowd craned his neck, but none moved closer. They waited. The horse's heads appeared on the edge of the town. Two Marshals rode on either side of the drawn wagon. Each carried a shotgun. A torch sat next to the wagon's driver. And then the wagon itself appeared. The crowd saw the seated figures in the back. It was them: The Rufus Buck Gang. The murderers. The rapists of white women. The nigger injuns who had terrorized them; the ones who'd sworn to drive white men from this land.

"It's them!"

Low, determined taunts swept through the crowd like mumbled prayers.

"Kill 'em all."

"Hang 'em." Spoken softly, loud enough for some to hear, but none too bold in case that human terror got free and came hunting vengeance—again—because that's what they did—hunt vengeance—for crimes not even criminal. Crimes that any white man just called living. That gang would hunt you and kill you just for living.

As the wagon neared, the crowd saw the shackles. With the sight of that constraining metal their courage exploded. Shouts echoed off the buildings. Faces instantly deformed with rage and hatred. Spittle flew and dripped on chins with each more violent oath. With the prisoners bound, the tables were turned and the Buck Gang were their victims now.

Then they saw the young faces. A fleeting lull descended. These were not the hardened men, the dime novel villains they all expected. These were boys, none of them out of his teens. They had been terrorized—made to question their rights as men—by children. The crowd exploded.

"Drag 'em off that cart."

"Hang 'em up!"

"Damn you to hell, Rufus Buck!"

A single gunshot cracked the air and then shots banged like firecrackers. The spitting, cursing crowd rushed the wagon.

"Filthy niggers!"

"We'll wipe you injuns outta here!"

The husband of Rosetta Hasson appeared. He walked and hopped alongside the wagon. He searched the four young faces, eyes lingering on one and then the other, all the while almost comically scurrying to keep abreast. Rufus Buck. He remembered him. The nigger; he remembered him too. He couldn't remember which one of them had done what to him—which bit of humiliation and degradation each had inflicted on him and his wife.

"Give him justice!" a woman screamed with tears in her eyes as she lay her hands on John Hasson's shoulders, a gesture he did not acknowledge, so enthralled was he with the men—the boys—who had so debased and brutalized him—who had made him watch.

Others took up the cry. "Give him justice!"

Grasping hands reached for the Bucks. The wagon tipped with the crowd's pressure and the horses bobbed their heads and swished their tails in irritation. The Marshals danced their horses to stand between the cart and the crowd. They sat remarkably unperturbed in their saddles, rifle barrels pointed in the air.

"What kind of men are you?" the crowd sneered at them.

"What if it was your wife?!"

The Marshals stared straight ahead as if surrounded by nothing more than grasping children. It was their job to see these prisoners safely to Ft. Smith, Arkansas to stand trial. Seeing it done right was a point of pride.

~ ~ ~

The procession passed him by. His daughter was not with them. The noise and blood lust continued down the street without him. He stood in the increasing quiet, screaming inside. He wondered if the news had been wrong. That idea buoyed him for a moment. Maybe she hadn't. Maybe it hadn't come down to this and he had not fallen so much farther and deeper than even he—who had fallen so far and so deep—could imagine. Clutching that ounce of hope, he walked to the Sheriff's office and asked if there were more.

The deputy said there was a girl; there would be no reprieve.

He waited in the office, dread like ants all over him, ignoring the stares and occasional titters of the two men inside.

Twenty minutes later, few noticed the single horse that followed the cart into town. Another Marshal rode it. A young girl about 13 years shared the Marshal's saddle. She was dirty, her blonde hair uncombed, dress torn, face smudged but even so, even filthy and tattered, one's first thought seized on her beauty. She gazed down the now-empty streets toward the invisible noise and commotion on the other side of town. She wondered if they were dead already.

The moment he heard the clop of horse's hooves, her father's heart beat wildly. He ran outside. He strained his eyes to see her and when he did, she looked neither scared nor sad. She just sat there, like nothing had happened, vacantly bedraggled and magnificent. Her nonchalance was purposeful, he thought, to provoke him. He swore not to give her the satisfaction.

The horse stopped. As she threw her leg over the saddle, all restraint abandoned him and he lunged at her as if she were prey. He grabbed her arm and yanked her to the ground. He slapped her viciously. He swung his outstretched arm like a two-by-four and slammed his open hand into her head and then swung it back to hit her with the back of it. He beat her with every ounce of strength as if he didn't care if it killed or cleansed them both. The girl lowered her head and raised her arm like a shield. She didn't make a sound.

The smacks echoed in the dark, empty Okmulgee street. Her father's loud, effortful grunts accompanied each. The satisfaction of hand meeting flesh was like food. He beat her until he could barely lift his arm. Then, exhausted, he fell to his knees. Even so he took another look at the girl and found the strength to raise his arm and land a final stinging blow to her now-bloodied head as if determined to destroy the last vestiges of beauty and grace that bespoke her resplendent beginnings. Panting through his teeth, on his knees, he did what he had not done in years—decades. Through his clenched toothed gasps for breath, he mumbled a prayer: "Dear God, give me the strength to kill her dead."

And then something extraordinary happened. He'd later say that since God had stopped listening a long time ago, the Devil got his prayer. In a haze he saw his wife's semblance beneath the girl's dirt and blood and half-matted hair. Momentarily startled, he stopped, and he glimpsed the past. He saw it bleed slowly into the present. He saw it all. He saw what had become of what should have been—several lifetimes worth of certainties, inevitabilities, pre-ordainments, all shriveled like carcasses and soiling his road from there to here. In Mississippi a lifetime ago, his 17 year-old self and teenage bride had lovingly envisaged the glories awaiting them and their children—the sons of plantation owners the girls would marry; the girls from good family the boys would court. There was no doubt about the world their children would inherit: columnar grandeur, ease and delegation, serviced by darkies happy to do it because it was their lot. And then the war—and his world became a process of ruthlessly picking the psychic scab of his status as a civilized man. At first it had been unbearable—watching his birthright retreat. But then his wife, the one through whose eyes he saw it fade, she died. Soon after, he stopped chasing it. He stopped striving for what was lost, and embraced what was at hand. Like a child, he learned to enjoy the methodical pain of revealing the raw skin - the true self - beneath the flimsy scab of civility. Standing in the street, whipping his daughter with all his might was the final rip. It was all gone. His beard unkempt, clothes filthy, a foul-smelling body with nothing to its name, the wound of raw living showed bright and pink for all the world to see and the girl he hit was its child. Standing in the street beating his girl for running off with that nigger renegade sealed his deliverance. They had won. The niggers had cost him his home, and now they befouled his daughter. It was the last barrier, the violation of the last shred of dignity he had, the last vestige of the past that he could possibly have held onto. And with that realization, his arm ridiculously aloft, he stopped. He staggered back.

She didn't move. She huddled, awaiting the next blow. She listened: a soundless 30 seconds save her father's heavy breathing before she dared sneak a look in his direction.

When she did, she saw him standing, arms akimbo, body tilted backwards as if he reveled in a windstorm. And then he laughed. He laughed and slapped his hands to his sides. He stomped the ground in lead-footed triumph and kicked a little dust in the air. After he settled down a moment, he looked hard at his daughter, and reeling like a drunk, he turned to walk away. Theodosia looked around. Two men smilingly stared from the doorway of the Sheriff's office like they had watched a medicine show, as if her blood and pain were funny. She realized that she still held her arms up to shield her face from nonexistent blows, so she quickly threw them to her sides and stood up straight. She stared at the two men. One of them put his hand on his privates and thrust his middle at her. The other doubled up laughing. She haughtily flicked her blonde hair back and stuck her tongue out at them before she turned to follow her father's fading figure into the darkness.

"Oh no you don't little girl," one of the men yelled as he tore off after her. Seeing him run, she bolted. She ran as fast as she could when a yank on her hair wrenched her head back and swept her bare feet from under her.

The man smiled down at her, panting. "You get to spend the night with us," he said as he pulled her up by her hair and dragged her back toward the jail.

~ ~ ~

As he did so often these days, Judge Parker sat awake in the middle of the night. The soft, pre-dawn knock at his door had not disturbed him. It would be, he knew, his young clerk, Virgil Purefoy. Anyone else would have raised holy hell to get him out of bed at this hour. There would have been pounding, soft shouts... Only Virgil would know, though Parker had never actually told him, that illness gave him sleepless nights; therefore mild taps would do. As he opened the door, Virgil spoke in a considerate whisper so as not to awaken the Judge's sleeping wife.

"I'm sorry to bother you, sir, but an urgent telegram."

Parker noted that Virgil was fully dressed, right down to his cravat. His full dress probably took no more time than a less idolatrous being's throwing on a dressing gown. Parker gestured him inside and tore the envelope. He scanned the note, then handed it to the almost-slavering boy, who read it hungrily.

"Excellent, sir," Virgil beamed. "Bringing them to justice will be a crowning glory for you."

Old and sick, Isaac Parker had reigned as judge, the mind of the jury, and the will of executioner throughout 74,000 miles of Indian Territory for nearly 20 years. By all appearances, he had triumphed. From the window of his upstairs office at the Ft. Smith, Arkansas courthouse, he now saw a bona fide city where there had been only badlands: Thriving stores, bustling liveries, electric streetcars and hotels—a city, yes... but still imbued with the taint of the wild. When he'd arrived here, 36 years old, the youngest Federal judge in the west, it had barely been a camp. Back then, you wouldn't move without a gun. There was no railroad; streets were mere muddied piles of horse dung reeking of the carelessly tossed pisspot. Lawlessness infected every transaction. Fist fight and gunfight erupted like wind gusts and just as unpredictably. Wild dogs bore themselves with more dignity than men in Indian Territory. Then God and the United States laid the burden of changing all of that on his young shoulders. He had accepted, and as a result, lawlessness had been restrained enough to allow commerce to flourish and opportunity to beckon hordes of white men and women to settle—illegally—the Territory. As his reward, in less than one year a new Courts Act would finish the job of stripping him of jurisdiction over the last remaining parts of his once vast domain. His court would end, his power would die with it.

Now, when he stared out of his courthouse window, all he surveyed, of which he could claim ownership as much as any man, filled him with ambivalence. He had yearned to turn the Indian Territory into something... more... something indefinably, unspecifiably superior... Yes, it was partly a young man's hubris—superior to everything that had come before. But he had never known exactly what he'd hoped to turn it into. Should it be the frontier's edge, like the Ohio of his birth, trembling with anticipation of civilization's embrace? Or should it be the frontier's essence, perpetually outside civility's sometimes-cold grasp? A city like St. Louis, or something entirely new? Young, he was a creature of duty and certainty, not imagination. So he did not think much on it. He never planned; he set no goals. He knew that God's hand had brought him here, and believed God's grace would guide him.

Over time he had lost his way. He believed in heaven; and when he arrived, he'd seen it in these lands—what God intended, the true Eden with which He'd entrusted mankind. Endless lands, limitless bounty, wild. The white men sprinkled amongst the Indians had adopted ways just as wild, but with dollops of malice and viciousness that reversion from civilization inevitably brought. But Parker knew that the return to civilization could put them to rights—his task. The Indians, less burdened with white men's civilities, having no aspiration toward them, no grounding in them and no guilt on bypassing them, seemed more at peace with the land they lived on and the lives they led. An elementalism. There was no striving in them. No desire to take this world from here to some indeterminate other place—to some heretofore undiscovered "there." Parker sometimes envied them their self-possession, but did not admit a gnawing sense that it might be more. They showed placidity amidst the hardships of death and illness, birth and survival, while he and his brethren warred ceaselessly with each. Eventually, with age, he learned to see strength in them (there was something downright Christian in their relentless acceptance, he decided—the quiet acceptance of God's will) and believed they would adapt to white men's strivings. Perhaps a civilized people on wild lands was his vision—the almost impossible contradiction settled in heavenly harmony and turning this place into some sort of blessed American Kingdom. Maybe that was what he'd wanted all along—to better God's work. Perhaps pride was his sin. He was doing God's will, he knew, but had he expected Divine result? What he saw in his courtroom and on the street beneath his office was not Divine. It was merely human. For him, toward the end of a life, that was not enough.

Awaiting atonement for his many sins against this place, he'd half-expected Rufus Buck. At first, he thought that Cherokee Bill had been the Judgment he dreaded, but Bill was a thief and a murderer—a sinfully charming and effective one, but nothing more. Parker believed in retribution; he did not believe in unpunished lies or unrequited obfuscations. He believed that deception and injustice literally bred—that they spawned and reproduced themselves to even worse effect. And in egregious cases, God in his wisdom made their bitter fruits manifest in flesh, and sinners suffered at the hands of their own misdeeds. When he heard of Buck's first warning, and when he suffered the torturous details of the rape of Rosetta Hasson, he knew that Buck was such a plague, more conjured than born.

"Congratulations, sir," Virgil called out as he opened the door to leave. "Their capture will be quite the feather in your cap."

"Quite a crowning glory," Parker replied obligatorily as he turned toward the stairs. "The final act," he said as he slowly ascended.

~ ~ ~

Rufus glared at his still-shackled hands and feet. Three others sat identically bound in the small, bare room. An occasional gunshot smacked outside. Above the muffled din of the growing, restless crowd, the odd curse or hollered threat flew through the second story window. Rufus looked at each of his men. Maoma angrily jerked at the chains as if sheer rage would break them. Sam worriedly watched Maoma, seeking clues on how to act to inoculate himself against accusations of cowardice—he had yet to explain his disappearance at the height of the battle. Short, black Luckey Davis sat dismally. His best friend, Lewis Davis, his brother in all but birth, had gone missing—probably dead, probably shot. Rufus smacked his fist against his thigh again and again until the sting turned to burning. They all should have died back there, he thought. Not to have done so was the coward's way. He berated himself for the same sins for which he had so recently reviled Cherokee Bill—another once-great man whom he loathed for crumbling in the end. The infamous Ned Christie had died with a gun in his hand, but the Rufus Buck Gang would be ripped apart by white dirt farmers and their women. At least their arrival in Okmulgee was something this town would never forget. The Marshals had to chase away the crowds at gunpoint. Those white farmers would have marched 100 miles—all the way to Muskogee—just to get their hands on him. From their screaming and spitting, from the outrage on their faces, Rufus knew he had hurt them, taken something precious—their inviolability—from them. He had given them a fleeting twinge of deadening wounds that people like his Creek Indian father and his Negro mother carried. They knew trembling fear because of him. They had, probably for the first time in their white lives, considered their own defeat because of him. While considering this small triumph, he drifted into sleep.

A few hours later, he woke to daylight and sounds of mayhem. He listened. He rolled to his feet and shuffled to the large window, his leg irons clanking raggedly. Down below, despite the hot August sun, came a river of horses and wagons as far as he could see, a swarm of people flowing toward the courthouse. More shots sounded. The screams and curses grew louder. It was a lynching mob. Sam, Luckey and Maoma watched Rufus. They felt his fear. They felt him fighting it.

"Let 'em come," Rufus said out loud to no one.

Maoma wrestled his chains even more desperately.

Panicked, Sam rose and shuffled furiously to the window. It was like something from a storybook. There were hundreds down there. The street was thick with them, all focused on the courthouse doors. Armed men stood before the building repeatedly pushing them back with their rifle barrels.

"They gonna let 'em have us!" the terrified Sam hollered. "They gonna let 'em lynch us!" He fell as he rushed from the window to the door, half crawling, chains clanging, to bang and scream for salvation. Looking over his shoulder, Rufus saw a tear against Luckey Davis' cheek, quickly wiped away. He knew what they were thinking. They all thought it was the end—that they would die now. Rufus watched his men like they were players on a stage, and wondered if they screamed and cried over death itself, or over the rough, bloody kind of dying that lynching meant. He wondered if he would see her again before he died. As the volume rose outside—as loud as running horses but dripping rage—he wondered if she would cry at his lynching for the love of him. Silent, stoic tears fell down Luckey's face. Sam continued pleading at the heavy wooden door. Maoma's body jerked and shuddered, rattling his chains in intermittent spasms of frustration and ineffectuality.

A key turned in the lock and the door swung open. On all fours, Sam skittered away.

Rufus pointed and laughed. "You look jus' like a monkey," he said to Sam.

Rifle aloft, barrel to the ceiling, Deputy N.B. Irwin stepped inside. Behind him stood Marshal Samuel Haynes, his rifle pointed at the Bucks.

"Nice to see you boys havin' a good time," Irwin said, noting the laugh. Before he could say another word, Maoma shouted amidst a cacophony of his own rattling chains.

"You gonna drag us out there for 'em ain't ya'? You gonna let 'em lynch us, you damned cowards!"

Irwin barely glanced at him and continued as if Maoma had not spoken. "Doubtless you boys seen the crowd outside. They got guns, clubs, torches and anything else they can carry. Hell, I saw some woman down there wavin' a skillet. An' we hear tell of folks headin' this way from all over."

He paused and glanced at them. He had their attention.

"Now our job is to get you all safe to Ft. Smith, to stand trial for what you done to them people. To do that, we gotta get you outta here. We talked it over, and best to do it after dark."

"You settin' us free?" Luckey Davis asked?

Irwin looked at him with something close to pity. "No son. We're gonna get you outta town after dark and on a train to Ft. Smith for trial. But we gotta do it without the folks out front hearin'—or the folks camped out all along the town. If they get to you, they gonna kill, and won't be much we can do about it. You're gonna have to be quiet, and carry your chains, real tight up against yourselves." He made a fist before his chest as if pulling up the chains attached to leg irons. "If you don't make no noise, we should be able to get you outta here safe."

All eyes stayed on him and he seemed satisfied. "We'll get y'all somethin' to eat before we go." He backed out of the room and closed the door. They all heard the key turn in the lock.

2

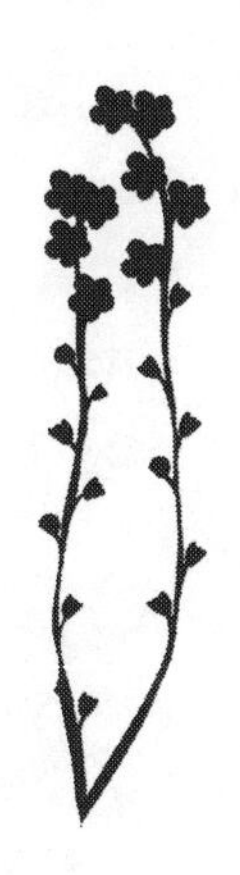

Since hearing of their capture, Parker had thought of little but the Bucks. The connections and coincidences seemed too numerous to ignore. In them, he sensed an historic pageant, a series of pre-destined events, momentous in their outcome, to which he was somehow central. He was desperate to understand his part.

His search led him to the Ft. Smith jail where he informed the surprised jailers that he wished to confer with Cherokee Bill. Just 20 years old, half-Negro like Buck, he and the judge had danced an exhausting legal waltz that wasn't yet finished. While awaiting the Supreme Court review of his richly deserved death sentence, Bill had attempted escape and murdered one of Parker's jailers. Parker had considered the Supreme Court decision to question his sentence a personal affront. He blamed its deadly aftermath more on the Court's incompetent and unjustifiable interference than on the man who pulled the trigger. In the wake of the Supreme Court's inexcusable meddling, Parker had made intemperate remarks and brandished the open insubordination that led, over time, to the dissolution of his court. He'd memorized what the Fort Smith Elevator had written because it justified his outrage:

> *"For the benefit of those who may not understand why Cherokee Bill was not hanged (why he was allowed to remain alive long enough to commit another brutal murder), we will say that his case was appealed to the Supreme Court of the United States upon what is known in the law as technicalities—little instruments sometimes used by lawyers to protect the rights of litigants but oftener used to defeat the ends of justice. It will remain there until the bald-headed and big-bellied respectables who compose that body get ready to look into its merits."*

The judges of the Supreme Court reviewed Parker's sentence as if something less than justice had been dispensed—as if that same justice had not almost miraculously dragged 74,000 square miles of Indian Territory towards civilization. Everyone knew Bill was a killer. He was just a different kind of one. Parker understood white violence: Rage, greed, sheer viciousness... any one could explain it. He understood Indian violence: A heathen people, their land threatened, uncivilized... he understood. But despite the innocent lives that myriad violence had taken, he preferred it to Negro docility. That was inhuman. It left one waiting, dreading the inevitably violent reaction to their state. He had turned Republican at the first secession and supported Lincoln throughout the war, but he understood why Southerners had scuttled Reconstruction. Handing black men the power to exact revenge for such treatment would have led to slaughter. Whenever a Negro outlaw faced his court, he wondered, 'Is this the one? Is this their violent Moses come to lead them from the desert?' He had to admit that he took particular interest in locking these up or sending them straight to hell by way of the hangman. It was his Christian duty to spare the civilized world the havoc they might wreak. Looking at the crimes behind Bill's shockingly young eyes, he saw that revenge. A half-breed: A white man's pride with a black man's history stoking the flames—a dangerous mix.

~ ~ ~

As Crawford Goldsby (aka Cherokee Bill) sat in his cell, Judge Parker, who had recently sentenced him to die, was the last person he expected to see. Bill noticed that the first floor prison noise had fallen from a holler to a hush. He wondered what had caused it, but he wasn't interested enough to get off of his cot to find out. He figured that if it concerned him, he'd know soon enough. And here it was. During their last meeting, Judge Parker had sat on his courtroom throne, solemnly stroking his long, white beard as he, almost absently, in a hail of verbose grandiosity, wished mercy on his soul and sentenced him to die. He was supposed to have hanged on June 25th. It was August.

He wasn't dead yet.

Cherokee Bill did not stand when the judge entered his cell. He saw no reason. He and the Judge had danced a dance, but for him, it was over. He would no more have risen for a discarded girl who sashayed past to flatter herself with more of his attentions.

"Get up you murderin' nigger!" the jailer yelled as he furiously raised his club and struck Goldsby. Always on guard, Bill twisted to let his back take the blow. The jailer raised his club for another lash when the Judge rushed forward.

"No. It's alright," Parker said as he raised a steadying hand. But the jailer tried to push past him, struggling with the frail Judge. The man's wild eyes frightened Parker, who wondered if Goldsby, the man he had twice sentenced to die, would bother to save him.

"He killed Larry Keating," the guard pleaded, as if begging Parker to let him continue beating the man who killed his fellow jailer. There might have been tears in his eyes. Embarrassed, Parker briefly looked away.

"It's alright. It's alright," Parker soothed as the man mastered himself and lowered his weapon. "Could you bring me a chair?" Parker asked, and the jailer gratefully disappeared to fetch one.

As the dangerous episode ended, Goldsby lay back on his cot and barely looked at Parker; he stared intently at the bottom of the bunk above his. Parker stooped a bit to see what was so interesting at that particular spot but couldn't see a thing without twisting himself into an undignified position. Annoyed, he straightened up. Whether Goldsby was purposefully behaving oddly or just doing what came naturally, Parker couldn't tell.

The jailer brought the chair; Parker sat. He had not been to the jail in some time, and while Bill stared in silence, he sat in awe of the copious splotches of fresh and dried tobacco-laden spittle dripping down and stuck to the walls. The smell was nowhere near as offensive as the old jail had been, but it remained stunning. A veritable tornado of flies hovered over the barely-covered waste bucket. How long and hard he had fought to get this jail built to replace the travesty that was the old one, and like so much resulting from long, hard fights, the result seemed commendable, but just shy of being worth all of that effort.

When he tore his eyes from the laden walls, he found Cherokee Bill looking straight at him.

"What can I do for you, Judge? Or you just come to let the jailer get a crack in?"

"You've heard about Buck?" Parker asked.

"Don't hear much here."

That was a lie. Buck had been imprisoned here a mere month ago and had befriended Bill. Some suspected Buck of helping to plan the attempted escape during which Bill had murdered the jailer. Parker wondered if Buck had played a part in that critical episode, the one that precipitated his fight with his judicial "betters," which accelerated his diminution in the eyes of what he reviled as "the legal community." Parker to Bill to Buck... the connections were too tight. He felt them tighten, cold like shackles.

And then the Judge surprised Bill.

"What did he want?" Parker asked.

This question had no subtext. In the months of courtrooms, lawyers and even the Supreme Court, Bill was unused to that. He read Judge Parker's face and saw nothing of subterfuge, only earnest inquiry. He rewarded forthrightness in kind.

"To be me," he said. "I think he wanted to be me."

"You've thought about him, too..." Parker said.

"To make things like they was before," Bill continued.

"What things?"

"For the Indians."

"He's almost still a boy. What does he know about how things were?"

"What he knows don't matter. What he thinks he knows... what he wants to know... What he dreams... That matters."

Parker closed his eyes and let his body slump with heaviness and guilt. "Had it not been for me, he never would have met you," he said. "I'd known his father, you see. I felt for his father, and trying to save the son, started all of this." The silence lingered. Parker sat, eyes closed, remembering... Bill watched him indulge the melodramatic pose for a while, and then lost interest.

"Don't get choked up about it," Bill replied, lying back and returning his gaze to the bunk above. "I'm sure he'd o' managed to kill someone without you."

~

One year prior, Parker's clerk had knocked. "John Buck and Samuel W. Brown," young Virgil Purefoy had announced.

Predictably, Purefoy dawdled, gawking for a moment before he closed the door. Equally predictably, Parker both embraced and resented the look on the young, glowing face—a look that said he eyed a commemorative statue brought miraculously to life. The son of a prominent Virginia landowner, he'd come all this way to clerk for the famous judge and see the last of both him, and the notorious Territories he ruled. He'd been here eight months and after all that time still regarded the Judge with a longing and tenderness, as if forever acknowledging the spectacle of vaporous history made magically and momentarily visible. Yes, the boy's making an historical romance of him amused the Judge. But it hurt. His end was on him. He didn't need reminding.

Virgil ushered into Parker's office Sam Brown, the mixed-blood Chief of the Euchee Indians and John Buck, a rancher and member of the Creek Council. Sam Brown's face wore a practiced, official's smile; John Buck's an emptiness that bespoke some level of inward devastation.

The Judge offered them refreshment. Each refused.

"We've come," Sam Brown began, as he lowered himself to his seat, "to ask for your help."

The judge interrupted to avoid acknowledging the gross diminution of his power and influence. "I know," he said. But I also know you've dispatched emissaries to Washington directly. How have they fared?"

Brown tilted his head, a man couching his words. "We've had respectful hearings wherever we've been welcomed, but nothing's changed. As you know, white intruders continue to flout the laws of land ownership, and the Dawes Commission plans are moving forward. What happened to the Cherokee can happen to us."

John Buck stared at a fixed point slightly ahead of him as if confounded. Parker doubted he had heard a word. Brown, on the other hand, understood everything; and it was at him that Parker grew angry. Why was Brown dragging him through this play-act that made his waning hurt like a disease of the bones? Brown knew good and well that Indian Territory was a Washington scrim elaborately hung to assuage its own conscience and mollify the Civilized Tribes. It was sheer as lace to everyone there. Parker dealt daily with the friction of the lie versus the reality, trying to make brown people like this silent John Buck understand that nobody meant what they said on the level of nations, that it was all a dumb-show, an elaborate theatrical staged to distract from the real goings-on backstage. The Indian Territory was attached, sold, divided and spoken for. There was already more than $1,000,000 worth of railroad property in it. As far as the Indians were concerned, it was gone. And Brown knew it. He was, after all, half white. He understood. He was prosperous, on his way to substantial fortune. He owned the trading post and post office at the Wealaka Mission, both of which relied on white trade. He understood: Bureaucracy, politics, coercion. It was in his blood. Brown took all the proper and necessary steps to protect his people, just as he took steps to protect himself. He had been instrumental in recruiting H.P. Callahan, a Bible-worshiping white man, to teach Indian children white men's ways at the Wealaka Mission School. He handled a meeting such as this, the bureaucratic dance and wrangle of it, like a white man—a mechanical matter of course. His job, he understood, was to be seen taking the appropriate steps—taking action, regardless of outcome. Results, in this case preordained, were neither here nor there. Through acts like installing Callahan at the school, perhaps he was trying to prepare his people for the inevitable. Parker wondered if men like Brown, to their own people, were heroes or traitors.

John Buck listened mute and seemingly unawares. Occasionally he'd shift his eyes to Parker. Parker always "felt" when he did so and turned. Each time, Buck held his gaze.

Full-blooded Indian, he had the face of a totem and Parker feared accusation in his expressionless placidity. The half-white Brown was not really Indian to him. Brown was a white man with a tinge. A part of Brown was like Parker. But Buck was different. He looked different. Parker assumed he thought different. He would not understand why white men relentlessly hounded his people across the land, wanting more and more and more of it. He simply would not understand such egregious taking. To him, it would be akin to some animal acquisitiveness that you would beat out of a dog but was, for some reason, allowed to run rampant in white men. Brown understood, as did Parker: They both understood that there was never enough, no such thing as too much. One could always have more. Wants, to them, were like breaths. Parker sympathized with the Indians, and could sometimes see their treatment as unjust, but he understood why they were treated as they were, and part of him saw no fault in it; yes, part of him saw destiny—not justice—but destiny in the dying, the loss, the winning and the godawful losing—it was the way of things. It was God's will.

Residing in Indian Territory, presiding over the criminals small and large who passed through his court every day, Parker had seen that there were different kinds of men and different ways of being. Buck was, through and through, an Indian. He was a kind who did not understand.

"We ask that you write to some of your friends in Washington," said Brown, "in the Congress, in the higher courts..." Parker cringed at that term, "higher courts" and hurried to interrupt again.

"I can certainly do that," he said. "However, my entreaties

may be less than influential. I can't tell you how many times I've made suggestions and requests of Washington only to be told by some functionary that they—not I—know best what is right for this Territory, despite the fact that I, alone, have borne the burden of justice here for over 20 years and singly brought the seeds and trappings of civilization..." He checked himself before he spoke recklessly. He did not need to further douse the embers of his career through public intemperance—regardless of how well deserved.

"What can we do?" The voice was so unexpected and matter-of-fact, Parker jumped. It was the heretofore-silent Buck, challenging Parker's self-involvement as well as his evasions. Again, Buck's eyes held him.

"Well," Parker hemmed and hesitated, "I suppose... continue to do what you've been doing. Appeal to all of the Indian authorities in Washington who will give you a hearing. Of course," he smiled, "I will appeal to any who will still listen to an old man."

"And what will that do?" Buck asked, unamused.

'Nothing,' would have been the only honest answer and the one Parker longed for the courage to give.

"We can hope for the best," Parker replied.

As furiously as Buck's eyes had seized him, they abandoned him and returned to their middle distance.

Subtly acknowledging that decorum had been punctured, Chief Brown rose and thanked the Judge for his time and the actions he would take on their behalf. The Judge extended his hand and Chief Brown shook it. As the Judge reached to shake Buck's hand, he balked at feeling young and needful, like a boy seeking an elder's approval.

"It may not be what we want," Parker said as he earnestly pumped Buck's hand, "but perhaps we can mold the changes more to our liking."

"In our own time, perhaps we could," Buck replied. "But the United States is in a rush."

~

To mitigate that rush, to ease his own relegation to the past, John Buck kept mementos. He would call his young son Rufus to him as he pulled the objects from the wall, ready to do his duty to pass the memories along; and every time he intended to speak from his heart, telling his boy what his history, his people's stories, and the relics on his wall had meant to him. Not just stories, not just the 'who' and the 'when' but conveying the soul and the feeling, the sense of why their losses meant so much.

John Buck would sit in a chair and eye the prizes, rubbing his rough hand gently on the bowl, and the necklace, and the piece of wood with small holes in it. He was surprised that Rufus liked this one the most. John Buck would blow through it and make tuneful whistles.

"It was part of a musical instrument," Buck explained to his son. "It belonged to a half-white man my father knew who fought in the Creek wars. He'd play this huge thing—these 'bagpipes' he called 'em—as warriors headed into battle. My father said they wailed like a ghost, like screaming and war cries."

Each time, he wanted to go on. He wanted to tell the story of his people with all of the passion, love and fury that he felt deep down inside him. But he could not. He could not speak the words. They choked him. The words he had to use, they acted like bile and he grew physically ill; and one word, with its infinite permutations ("lost" "loss" "gone"), sounded like bells clanging deafeningly in his head.

"Lost."

So John Buck told brief, disjointed stories, and then put the mysteriously sacred objects of triumph and memory back on their hangers, back on their shelves, and simply walked away.

Rufus would sit and ogle them long after. His father said they would one day be his. The memories would be his. He longed to invest them with the same near mystical import he gleaned from his father's face and silence, the profound melancholy and ancient hurt that they obviously held, the key to which his father—for lack of desire or will, or due to Rufus' own lack of worthiness—the key to which his father never shared. As the boy grew older, his father no longer called him for these sessions. But Rufus occasionally found him communing with his relics. Rufus would sit near his father, unacknowledged, and silently watch.

Years later, in 1894, John Buck took 16 year-old Rufus to Tahlequah to see the government pay out money to the neighboring Cherokee. The tribe had sold their land to the United States, but instead of the tribe getting the money, each Cherokee man and woman would get $265.70. His father couldn't believe it. The tribe would get nothing. He told Rufus he expected the same to happen to the Creeks. Rufus figured his father wanted to see what it was like.

Rufus looked forward to the trip. He imagined solitude and the road working wonders between him and his father.

There would be nothing to do but talk. He imagined finally learning about his father's life and his father's father's. He imagined becoming a proud son and a source of pride.

Though the trip began in silence, he kept high hopes.

"Cherokee Bill's a Cherokee," Rufus said, priming the pump. "I bet he'll come to get the money. I been readin' about him."

His father did not respond. Eyes fixed on the road, he paid no mind to the hot sun, to the blanched grass that stretched to the foothills or to the oak trees that dotted them. A wake of buzzards circled nearby; something big was dead. Rufus scrambled for topics that might engage his father.

"How come Ma didn't come?" he asked, though he hadn't wanted her to. His father did not answer.

Before the trip, Rufus had asked his mother, "How come Pa don't talk no more?" She'd chastised him with, "You lucky you got him. I didn't have a Daddy. What are you complainin' about?"

"If you didn't have a Daddy," Rufus replied, "does that mean I'm like Jesus?" She slapped him and never told him why. He never asked her about Jesus again.

Over time, in bits and pieces, he learned more about his mother's past than he knew about his father's: that her mother had been a Negro slave of the Lower Creeks back in Georgia, before the Creeks were forced to relocate to the Indian Territories. These Creeks did not treat black slaves the way white folks did. He learned that the Lower Creeks treated slaves like regular people. Didn't beat them; sometimes even married them. But when the Creeks got marched to the Territories, a white man bought his grandma. After that, it was all blood and screaming as a white man's slave. As such, she heard crying and moaning for days on end to the point she thought she'd lose her mind. She could have killed the grieving mothers and widows, the whipped and the maimed, just to silence the inescapable, audible proof that she lived amidst such bottomless pain.

When she found a suitable man, she took months convincing him to run away with her, knowing full well that they would probably die, or wind up whipped or mutilated, but she didn't care. It shocked her, but she didn't care. It had never occurred to her that she would laughingly die and consider her own death vengeance against her killer. That's because she had never been owned like this.

So they ran. They ran toward Indian Territory where Negroes lived free. Her man got caught so that she could go on. She never knew what happened to him. She refused to think about it. She made it to the Indian Territory, and there she died giving birth to a girl six months later—giving birth to Rufus Buck's mother. So his mother had no parents. The Creeks raised her. Eventually, she married one. The Creeks told her what had happened to her mother and hers before. Their peoples' wounds were linked and the Creeks considered it their duty tell her about them. They explained how her mother had lived among them and the distinctions between being a Lower Creek slave and a white man's. But despite their protestations, the slaveries were not distinct to Iona Buck. If her mother had never been a Creek slave—if the Creeks had not owned her and sold her, the whites never would have gotten their hands on her. Rufus' mother had been conceived within a crime and raised among, and grateful to a people that some part of her still considered criminals—a conundrum like a tumor inside her, large enough to cause discomfort, but small enough to grow accustomed to—not worth the pain and risk of removal.

"There ain't nothin' you can do," she told Rufus when he asked about his father. "These Creeks keep tryin', but your father knows better." She paused a moment, watching the chickens meander and peck as she scattered feed. "White folks want what they want," she said to no one in particular. "They get what they get."

"Ain't you gonna say nothin'?" Rufus finally blurted at his father on the road to Tahlequah.

"I'm done talkin'," his father said.

They rode for eight more hours in silence. The wagon's creak, the snorting horses, the summer stillness, that's all Rufus heard.

They camped that night and he dreamed that angels came in song and sound and gently took him up to heaven. It looked a lot like home, but felt more beautiful than the home he knew, or any he'd ever imagined.

When his father woke him, it was already hot. The night had never cooled. They climbed on the wagon and in the span of a couple of hours, saw more people than they had seen during the whole trip. By the middle of the morning, they were just two among a moving crowd larger and more epic than any Rufus had ever seen. All these men and women, all these horses and wagons with one single purpose, with one destination… how sweet the goal must be to lure so many… Surely a promised land... Sweat blackened men's collars and shirts while many slid increasingly filthy sleeves and handkerchiefs across their faces. Dust thrown up everywhere by all the wagons and horses slogging slowly forward. Every kind of person, mule, buggy and conveyance crammed up together and eagerly crawling their way into Tahlequah.

John Buck had imagined what he would see there—a funereal scene in which the Cherokee took slips of paper in exchange for their future and their past. On faces he thought he'd see a sadness bone deep, something that touched him to his soul and thus let him truly understand whatever it was that had silenced him, and understanding, let him articulate and pass to his son what had been lost instead of suffering this mute rot of anger and want and fear inside him. He imagined an eerie silence, none daring refuse such money but all acknowledging the death of tribal ways that its taking represented. Maybe he just wanted permission to stop hoping. He imagined tear-stained dollars as the Cherokee marched back to their homes, both richer and less than they had been when they arrived.

At first it was a trickle. John and Rufus Buck came upon and passed a few wagons, some Indians on foot, a few on horseback, and then more, and then still more. Soon, the road was like a cattle drive of people. Most looked Cherokee, but some looked like white men; you didn't have to be all Cherokee to get the money. Badge-wearing white, colored, and Indian Marshals rode swiftly through the crowds, their rifles aloft, hustling people out of their way. Closer to Tahlequah, occasional white men in suits stood on the sides of the road in groups of two or three, commenting on the living diorama that passed before them as if it were a grand parade. Must have been Indian bureau men, John thought, surveying the tangible results of their work. Wheels broke and people labored in the road to fix them as the crowds coursed around them like water around a rock. Pissing men dotted the roadsides like statuary.

Medicine wagons hollered about a cure for this or that and others screamed that they had whiskey—all kinds of whiskey. Whiskey was illegal in Indian Territory, but nobody cared that day. One wagon passed by full of jugglers with painted faces and acrobats in tights. Another passed dripping with whores all dolled up and beckoning every man who looked. It was like the carnival had come to town. This is what John Buck had come to see—how it was done; how yet another piece of you falls away in exchange for handfuls of nothing.

He had wanted Rufus to see it. He didn't know why, not specifically. There was no lesson he could articulate that he wanted the boy to learn. There wasn't any practical reason why he should have come. But the boy had to… absorb. He had to befriend what was dying for the Cherokee, hold its hand and listen to its deathbed ramblings, and then learn to exist in the void of what was left when it happened to the Creeks, as John Buck knew it would. John had no idea what that meant or how to do it, but he had seen and thought too much of one way of living to change now, and it was killing him. Maybe it wasn't too late for his son.

Buck remembered the day back in 1893—the precursor to this spectacle, another of his pointless treks of witness: 100,000 white men stood, sat on horseback and rode in wagons, sweating in the heat and epic dust of the Cherokee Strip to race for 42,000 plots of land. The land belonged to the Cherokee, and the United States first used it to settle friendly Indians; and then the cattlemen wanted it for grazing, so eventually the government bought it to feed its voracious appetite for the earth itself. In exchange for this land, the government would pay money—not to the Cherokee tribe as a whole, as traditional and right dictated, but to each individual member—every man and every woman. To Buck, that was like buying a house and splitting the money evenly between the man, his wife, and each child and telling them all to go their separate ways. It was the end of the tribe as their collective soul. It was one of many endings. So in '93, John Buck watched as they shot off a gun and the unimaginable throng of white men, women, and children all scrambled for their piece of Cherokee heaven, for which each Cherokee man, woman and child would later be paid $265.70. There were more would-be white settlers than there were potential homesteads. Most got nothing. At the end of the day, John Buck rode among them as they lay exhausted with the dust stuck to their sunburnt, sweaty white faces. He watched as they wept in the dirt at not being fast enough, hungry enough, maybe just not white enough to get a piece of Cherokee land.

And here, today, one year later, each Cherokee lined up to receive his little bit of the payment for the tribe's land so valiantly raced for one year earlier. Each one. $265.70. If you could prove you had some Cherokee in you, you got the money, but you had to go to Tahlequah in Cherokee country to collect it. John Buck went to see it happen to the Cherokee, knowing that a similar day would come for the Creeks.

Off in the distance, rifle stocks stuck up in the air like trees. A little forest of them, all protecting the millions getting handed out, $265.70 at a time. There were lines and lines of people waiting for it. Others lined up to take it from them. Whiskey peddlers swarmed like flies. Gamblers set up tables right out in the open. Men and women no sooner got the money in hand than they went off to drink it and lose it at cards. John

Buck stopped the wagon and watched from the back of the crowd. Some emerged from the thick of it, counting their bills when waiting debt collectors swooped in to take it from them. One woman fought like hell. "This is Cherokee money!" she yelled, kicking and swinging at the two men who pried her fingers open to take the crushed cash. A fiddler played while some white folks danced in the middle of the crowd. One man and woman walked free of the throng looking so sad, like they had just buried something—looking like John had expected all of them look. But most didn't. The whole plain was like a funeral hidden behind a festival, something cheerless hiding in a saloon. John never once looked at his son sitting beside him. He was so amazed and appalled at what he saw himself that he barely thought of Rufus.

Buck lifted the reins and clicked his tongue. The horse woke up and pulled the wagon, this time against all the people still streaming into Tahlequah for their $265.70.

John Buck swore that it was the last lacerating piece of State theater he would force himself to witness. Rufus never uttered a sound. They rode home in silence. What happened was never mentioned between them.

3

"We behold the face of nature bright with gladness, we often see superabundance of food; we do not see, or we forget that the birds which are idly singing round us mostly live on insects or seeds, and are thus constantly destroying life; or we forget how largely these songsters, or their eggs, or their nestlings, are destroyed by birds and beasts of prey;"

- Charles Darwin
"The Origin of Species"

On the day of his expulsion from the Wealaka Mission School for Indian Children, Rufus hid lurid pamphlets on spectacular crimes and criminals inside of his Bible. He had long reveled in the pamphlets' florid imaginings of the whisky peddlers, bank robbers and cattle thieves for which Indian Territory was famous. The Indian and Negro outlaws were as renowned as any. "The very sight of the ruthless red Indian in all of his Godlessness," he read, "causes women to shriek, and grown men to flee for the safety of numbers with which to beat back the barbarisms he gleefully inflicts. Torture, scalping, and ravishment of women are the arrows in his heathenish quiver, and he shoots them straight and true."

Rufus had not known.

He excelled at reading at the Mission School owned by Sam Brown, the mixed-blood Chief of the Euchee Indians. At Brown's behest, S.P. Callahan managed the school as superintendent and chief instructor. He brought an impressive eastern pedigree—Yale University some said with little more evidence than the splendid, shiny black suit he always wore. Each day he paced the room full of black and brown faces caressing the long words rolling off of his tongue, silently, yet persistently acknowledging his superiority to all of his surroundings and taking shameless pride in his ability to elevate them—if not to his level then at least to a level at which intercourse with them would not demean him.

He taught the Bible, and his Indian students grew stronger and more disciplined through the endless repetitions, forced recitations and appropriate punishment for insufficient deference. He forbad the speaking of Creek or any other Indian language. His black riding stick stood at the ready to beat any student caught doing so—in class or on the playground—or committing any other of the myriad infractions that reinforced the savagery of their natural state and surroundings and undid his noble work of civilizing them.

"I may not be able to make you white," he told them. "But I can make you act like it." He paused to knock a boy on the head with the black whip for paying insufficient attention.

That the Creek Council had hired him to civilize these children proved his theory that the sloughing off of savagery and heathenism were primal human drives. They needed only prodding and the lash to show themselves. His whip was his prod, the Bible his lash. These young ones would be better men than their fathers had been. They would be fit to live alongside white men. They would be called Christians.

Rufus lapped up every dime novel he could find about Cherokee Bill, who, he had read, once robbed every store from one end of the town of Lenapal to the other. Half Negro, Half Cherokee, he rode with Bill Cook and killed a Deputy with a shotgun from the back of a galloping horse. They say he shot a man during a robbery because he didn't like the look in his eye. Bill was his favorite, the last of the living legends.

Another favorite: Ned Christie, a full-blooded Cherokee. Rufus saw himself as sharpshooter, like Christie, blacksmith and gunsmith, like Christie, and like him, a law-abiding citizen tending home and hearth until viciously pursued for a murder he did not commit, from which time he had no choice but to run and wander—alone, hardening, honing his skills and keeping all law at bay through Indian know-how and superior cunning. Little did the public know that he was a good man. How tragic, Rufus thought, that they would only know the lawman's lie of the ruthless murderer. A deadeye, he could have easily killed his pursuers, but he did not. He only shot to injure them. Rufus smiled at that, because, unlike Christie, he would have known the effect his mercy would have on the cowardly lawmen. Rufus would have known that instead of acknowledging his kindness, they would feel humiliated and multiply their efforts to kill him dead—a good, honest man who dared to spare their sorry lives.

Later, he thought, the smile had given him away—the smile as he imagined himself as Ned Christie, alone in a small cabin, successfully fighting off a phalanx of law with only his single rifle—until the cowards used dynamite to blow the wall off the cabin. And then he saw his own dead body, as if from heaven, laid out just as Ned Christie's had been. He watched the son of the lawman he was accused of killing slowly approach and empty a revolver into his still-fresh corpse. He watched crowds surround his body on the steps of the Federal Courthouse in Fort Smith (where he'd been displayed for the instruction and edification of local school children.) He saw the children eye him, and knew that in their minds his corpse was not a warning, but a call.

To the background noise of Callahan's mellifluous drone, Rufus imagined the epic gunfight during Cherokee Bill's escape from Tahlequah, where he'd gone to collect his $265.70 in Cherokee money. Rufus had seen the spot with his very own eyes, and was vividly dreaming the raucous, smoke-filled scene when Callahan's whip sent fire down his cheek. He raised his hand at the painful sting. Blood seeped through his fingers. Without thinking he jumped to his feet. Callahan stood impossibly erect—to the point of leaning backwards—and stared contemptuously down at him.

"The very sight of the ruthless red Indian in all of his Godlessness," Rufus had read. At least his color should have struck fear, as it did with Christie and Cherokee Bill, but it didn't. Callahan showed none. It was the man's assuredness that galled Rufus. The lack of any fear; the assurance that he had the right to dole out pain without consequence. So in an instant, Rufus grabbed the stick from Callahan's hand, and as if hurling a rock, slashed him with it. The class gasped. Callahan grabbed for the weapon. Rufus pushed the grasping hands away and they struggled like children for the little black stick until Rufus finally snatched it and threw it to the corner of the room.

"Get out!" Callahan screamed, shaking with rage and pointing to the door.

Rufus stood his ground—sixteen and almost eye-to-eye, he felt power for the first time.

Callahan lurched toward him. Rufus ripped a knife from his pocket and held its blade aloft. It split Callahan's image. The instructor stopped short.

"You are sin," Callahan said, low and calm. "You are savage, and there is no putting you to rights."

"That's all you got now, words?" Rufus taunted.

Callahan stepped back. "Look at him, all of you. This is one that no one can save. He will live in gutters, like a dog and God will turn his back on him..."

Rufus wiped the blood from his face and slowly turned to go. Callahan followed, step for step, haranguing as if exorcising demons from the soul of the room. He thundered, *'You became filled with violence within, And you sinned; Therefore I cast you as a profane thing Out of the mountain of God.*"

Rufus was 100 yards away before he heard no more of that voice. He didn't know why, but for the first time knew that such words didn't matter, that they could not brand him.

It was his first small step toward his destiny.

He didn't go home—not because he dreaded his father's reaction. His father would accept it as he accepted everything—as another defeat. Rufus swore that if someone showed up with bagfuls of money, his father would moan. It was as if some gut-shot loss had possessed every inch of him, not to be banished by any joy, no matter how great. Rufus simply didn't want to be the cause of yet more whiskey-soaked self-pity.

He heard old-timers say that Tulsey Town used to be a little nothing of a place. Then, they said, the railroad came and immediately began doing what it still did with ever-increasing vigor. Rufus hitched a ride from Okmulgee to watch as the Tulsey trains disgorged white folks and livestock—inhaling lumber in return. He watched the long, black cars arrive in clouds of screeching noise and black smoke. Freight doors thundered open, ramps slapped the ground, Indian and white men shunted cattle in and out of the cars, hollering, whips cracking, the cows lowing endlessly. Further down the train, white men and women done up in finery stepped out of the passenger cars. These were the fancy types who came before the Creek council for permits to log and graze the land.

Another car spat plainer folk. Sun-darkened men in sweat-stained shirts, women in soiled tops and simple skirts with caps and kerchiefs on their heads. Faces smudged, dirty children in tow, they eyed their new surroundings with hope and trepidation, wondering if this would be the place where they could fulfill the vague promise of "better and more," embedded in their minds as firmly as God's existence.

Rufus' gaze lingered on the Dandies. Seeing them next to the dull men and women was like brightness and daylight compared to dirt. Compared to the Indians and freedmen, they were big, light, brilliant birds that could fly away on a wind if they wanted. He felt a knot in his stomach, fearing that his short, dark self could not compare to them. Maybe that was what his father wanted him to learn by sending him to Callahan's school... what he didn't have the heart to tell him—that they had won because they were better. He shoved the thought to the back of his mind.

~

As he stared at his shackles and chains, the Sunday morning train slowed at the Fort Smith station. All night, throughout the tense, stealthy flight from the wailing lynch mobs in Okmulgee, Rufus had searched his past and identified more and more signs and signals that had set him on his current course—the road that had taken him so close to being a great man. The Ft. Smith church bells tolled for his victims. He counted the deep, mournful chimes. They reminded him of similar tinnier, less sonorous bells that again linked his past to his present and his inevitable future because on most Sundays for the first twelve years of his life his mother had said, "Let's go see the people," as she donned her best dress and her plain, black hat with bright feathers on it. On those days, John Buck had the wagon hitched and ready and lifted the boy up into his seat before he patted the horses to send them down the road. Rufus waved goodbye until his arm ached. Rufus liked these trips because during them, his mother was different. She wore a small smile instead of the usual pinched look.

"How come you don't live here?" he asked her as they entered the freedman town full of black faces to the sounds of the high church bell.

"Your Daddy's Creek," she said. "But if my Mama had lived, this probably where I'd be." She looked down at her son and smiled. "On Sundays it gets to be."

As usual, the preacher stood in front of the small congregation, the worshippers on their feet before empty chairs. Rufus liked the music sung to hand claps. But this day, suddenly, shockingly, a woman screamed as if on fire and threw her hands up in the air.

"Jesus!" she hollered, as if he had threatened her. "Jesus! Oh Jesus, JESUS!" She flew forward and others cleared a path and pushed her toward the preacher as if her wildness merited an honored place.

"The spirit of the Lord is with us today," the preacher calmly stated with a beatific smile as he opened his arms to the wailing woman as if to showcase her outrageous gyrations and accent her shattering yelps. The singing rose in volume and intensity.

Rufus stared at the picture of the ethereal, blonde Jesus against the rough, wooden wall and wondered what He had done to the woman to make her scream and holler so. Had this Jesus invaded her like some frantic demon and if so, what message was so vital that it made the woman spit and spasm so violently to be heard?

Then he saw her. A vision. And the moment he did, he knew his world had changed.

She stood serenely before the congregation. She looked directly at him, unmoved by the woman's wild exclamations—oblivious to the congregants' raucous song. In a white, flowing robe against skin almost as white, she beckoned him, as calm as the heavens themselves. Eyes bluer than any sky. Without sound, without motion, she called him. He felt her draw on what must have been his soul. He had never felt a pull so deep and strong before. He yearned to follow, but something held him back. Despite her blissful mien, there was darkness in her. She bespoke something too big and ponderous for his young self to bear. It might crush him, he thought. It was too much. In his head, in words he knew that only she could hear, he told her that he could not come to her, could not join her as the woman writhing joined her Jesus, not now, not yet. He was scared to be an Angel's chosen one.

And then, as if rebuffed, the angel disappeared. The screaming woman fell to the ground, moaning and writhing, shaking spasmodically, mumbling, "Jesus, Jesus, take me, Jesus..."

He stared at the flailing figure transfixed. He knew that his dangerous Angel, not the humdrum Jesus, had conjured such fearsome exultation.

Every subsequent Sunday he waited. He stared at the woman who had called out before, awaiting her next effusion, a sign of the presence of his Angel. The woman swayed and muttered, but nothing more. He closed his eyes and pictured her in place of the Jesus on the wall, but his Angel did not reappear.

Young, he forgot her over time.

And then, almost three years hence, she returned. It was after his mother stopped going to the freedman town to worship her God. She never said why she stopped and Rufus never asked her. It was after the pinched look overtook her face, and after his father began to act as if desperately pondering the unfathomable, the comprehension of which all things—even his life—depended.

Sitting chained on the train to Ft. Smith, his heart quickened as he recalled the dream, and how She spoke to him of destiny. He sighed and smiled with such pleasure that his guards came forward. One grabbed his wrists to check his chains. He continued to smile as he remembered the tenderness with which she'd touched his face and hair. He had felt her. Soft, white skin against his. He felt her everywhere. It was her gift. She showed him signs. She filled his head with echoes and images. He saw Callahan's face and heard his deep, stentorian voice intoning tales of Biblical salvation. He saw Creeks outfitted for battle thundering forward, the hooves of hundreds of horses literally shaking the earth beneath his dream, and he heard a haunted, unearthly sound above the din he knew to be the wail of the "bagpipes." Her hand caressed his arms and then his chest. He felt their light touch telegraph her warmth through the hair on his thighs and then his manhood submerged into warmth and wetness like the flesh of heaven itself. In his dreams he rose from the bed in delight and ecstasy, bathed in a slow, honeyed warmth as lustrous as the Angel's hair.

He woke convulsing. Warm, slick goo shot prodigiously forth. He lay panting and confused, exhausted with satisfaction both celestial and demonic. He stared at and fingered the mucousy porridge he'd spilled from his belly to his chin. From the other boys' tales, he realized what had happened, but none had mentioned Her. If She was his alone, he figured he was truly blessed, her Chosen One.

He wanted to run outside and tell the world, but knew better. He sensed that his was a savage Angel who pleasured, but terrorized as well. Her missives were not to be ignored or thoughtlessly cast about. But how to read them? He jumped from his bed and ran to the kitchen, grabbed a can of lard and returned to his room. He slathered his member and stroked it furiously, eyes closed to conjure the Angel again. He conjured and he conjured with all his might, and again the liquid splurged into his hand, but alas, no heavenly being and what had been shudders were mere vibrations compared to the euphonic quakes that She had induced. So he tried again. He closed his eyes and pictured her white flesh beneath the flowing gown. Again the warm liquid, the vague sensations, but no heavenly host. His hands and half his arms shone with lard and all around his privates gleamed like polished bronzed but still he tried again, despite the growing pain. It barely throbbed to the beat of his heart, so he struggled more mightily until he scratched a spot of blood on the tip. He panted from the effort and the pain seared with each stroke, but this was his Temple.

It was the church through which almighty God had spoken and through which He had sent his minion to mark Buck's destiny, and it was his duty to sing praise and hosannas to Her viscous and agonizing Glory until she made her purpose clear. He tried, but the pain grew too great. Beaded with sweat, his arms fell limply to his sides as he sat on the edge of his bed, knowing that he would await Her return like a bride awaits her groom, like a prophet his God.

~ ~ ~

Bill Swain's stubborn mare pulled his cart through the pre-dawn light. He reluctantly rode to Fort Smith where they had taken his daughter. He had no choice. The letter... the goddamned letter demanded it. Like a too-familiar song the words filled his head as the sun rose and his aching back bounced on the wagon's wooden seat. He eyed the rising sun and the morning's first soaring birds, but the song played on. He was heading there, wasn't that enough? He was doing his duty, as demanded. He had fallen as low as any white man could... Wasn't that enough for her?

"God mutherfuckin' dammit to HELL!" he screamed at the golden emptiness. The mare ignored his outburst. He rifled the saddlebag sitting next to him and removed the creased, torn papers. He carefully unfolded them. They were dreaded, but sacred nonetheless. Even after all these years, each time he opened it something in him hoped that magic had occurred and he would read something different. But again, the letter had not changed. Not since he last read it, not since he'd first read it 13 years ago. But he kept at it. He kept reading it as if the letters would dance on the page and land in different patterns, thus rewriting his life and revealing him, to his own delight, to be a better man.

To My husband, Bill Swain, at the time of my death,

The world is broken and I can no longer stumble through it. The spasms are like a devil inside me. I am too old. I should have been spared this. But if the child I prayed I would never bear lives, I hope it is a boy so he can go off and make his own way when he is still young. The colored woman attending says that it won't be much longer. There's something wrong. The baby is not right inside me. I've seen women's birthing pains and this is not like them. This pain is God's curse. This hellfire inside an old woman is not bringing life. It is a herald and it is saying that my time has come and that my passage will not be easy. I do not believe that I am to blame for the life I have led, but if I have lived poorly enough to deserve this tortured path to God's infinite mercy, I accept it in the name of the Lord.

I had believed that you were a good man. To my youth-blinded eyes you, barely older than I, were brave and strong as you took the uniform to fight. You made me feel that an army of men so honorable and courageous could not fail against those who would steal from us what we had made and what was ours by right. So I became a child bride to a near-child husband. At first, your letters filled me with pride. And later, I did not believe the stories of failure and loss because you could not fail and you could not lose.

To find you cowering, stinking of your own filth—a deserter, not a scratch on you—it was the day I began my long, slow dying. I saw the look on old Celia's black face as she stared down at you. All the niggers were talking their freedom and our loss and she looked at you with triumph in her eyes. I marched right over to her and slapped it out of them. Then she did the unspeakable. She raised her hand and struck me. You watched. That nigger slapped my face, and then slapped it again and then again until I knelt on the ground cowering from her nigger strength above and beyond that of any white woman. Had there been any man left in you, you would have risen and whipped the skin off her back before you killed her dead and then hung her up for the others to learn a lesson. But you sat whimpering with your hands across your head like it was you she beat. She ran off that day and took all the young ones with her. They knew we were done. They could smell your fear. Like animals, they knew defeat when they saw it.

I left you lying there. After three days, when you did not come out, I returned to find you just as I had left you, but now half-dead from lack of food or water. And like a fool I dragged you outside. I washed the filth from you. I fed you spoonful by spoonful, and seeing the nothing behind your eyes, almost began to feel sorry for you. I started to pray that you would come back to me the man I had married and who had promised me a life of plenty and contentment under God's watchful eye.

The day the war ended was the day you looked at me, and I could tell that you saw me and knew me, and I could have shouted for joy. I ran toward you and kissed your face and inside I sang praise to merciful God. And then you grabbed me. With gritted teeth you tore my dress. You ripped the buttons free and with violence pulled the seams apart. Like a merciless animal you tore everything from me, threw me to the floor and took me by violence until I bled. When you were spent, I lay sobbing. You rose and said, "Get up. We got work to do."

You dragged me to the fields and hoed some rows and threw some seeds like they would come up overnight. When they did not, you spat and cursed me, as if it had been my fault. When old Remmie, the only nigger left on the place, tried to tell you how to make crops grow, you took a shovel and beat him half to death screaming that you were a white man and no nigger had anything to tell a white man. You sold everything for a carpetbagger's pittance. I asked you where we would go and how we would live. You never answered.

I could have forgiven you your cowardice. I

could have forgiven your violence if you had been willing to build another man from the ashes that you had become. But I realized that this animal before me was what you truly were. Money and ease had veiled it, that's all. They were your masks. I think you knew it too, and that is why you walked about in constant rage, like a large, willful child, breaking things, breaking me, as if to make all about you as broken as you were. I should have seen. It was my own doing. I was blinded. I could not have imagined a war and all the blood. I could not have imagined a nigger striking me and living to tell. I did not imagine a savage behind the mask of a man. Our world was gone, and you did not have the strength to build another. That is why I die with hatred for you in my heart. Had you shown an ounce of resolution, I could have followed you. I could have matched you stride for stride. But you left me with nothing. Seven years after the war, you had spent it all. You sent me to beg from those who still had something or were building something new. You made me face the pity. "Poor Constance," you could see in their eyes. "It would have been better if Bill Swain had died in the war." But I got us food to eat. If you had stayed, if your pride and your ignorance had not prevented it, we could have hired niggers and had everything back again. You could have become yourself again. You could have donned the mask and I would have pretended it had never slipped. I would have convinced myself that nothing lay beneath. But admitting what you could not do and learning new ways was too much for you. You preferred to burn it all to ashes. So we wandered. From place to place when even neighbors' pity would not put bread on our table, down to shacks and huts and finally here, my deathbed, where I hear the hammers clang on the railroad tracks. You wield one. But I suppose at least you do not have to ask how that is done. Even in death I will never forgive you for marrying me.

If this child lives, I pity it. If it is a boy, name him Blaine. If it is a girl, call her Theodosia. When the child is old enough to read—if, by then, there is any bit of a man left in you—let them read this letter. Have the courage to show them what you did to me. Let them look on you and despise you for it as I do. Show them how you became nothing and dragged their mother, a helpless woman, into shacks and gutters that stole the life from her.

I cannot bear this agony. What is yours is tearing me apart inside. I welcome death but God won't even take me now. It would serve you well if when I die, the child be stillborn. Let the midwife hand you the corpses you have made.

~

You lived according to your station—that's all Bill Swain had known when the war began—and his station had been good, pre-ordained like his sex or his skin. The world was his and there was no need to question any part of it.

He felt palpable pride as he rode with his regiment to certain victory. The sight of men united in noble purpose, himself a young officer among them—it was a culmination of his vision of himself. When the blood began to flow, it was the price to be paid and he took it in stride... a limb, a life... it was worth it. He knew that he would proudly shed blood for the cause, which was just; and he felt in his soul that the right and justice of it would see him triumphantly through.

Only at Vicksburg did he falter. Loss did it, the one thing that he had not imagined and could never have envisioned. The prospect of loss changed everything. Death had enveloped him since the beginning of the war, but being forced to consider the possibility of loss, seeing defeat written in the dirt of Confederate soldier's faces, that's when everything he needed vanished: the promise of the resurrection of the dead; the undoubted execution of God's almighty will; the certainty of his place in this world... They all disappeared. Starving and waiting for the Union troops to overrun them, justice sat on the other side of General Pemberton's line. It sat deep in the Mississippi's waters where union gunboats spat flesh-shattering fire. All of his rights and privileges lay across the river on the enemy's side. He couldn't reach them. It was as if they had ripped out his soul, the God-given part that makes one human... the privilege. After that happens, the spilled blood looks different. No longer imbued with nobility, it's just red and ghastly. The severed arm is a ragged sheath of pulpish flesh with a shattered bone protruding and not a noble sacrifice; the side of a body ripped away exposing bleached ribs and loose entrails like lifeless worms is the devil's doing, not

God's. Low and ignominious. With victors at the gates, the blood and bones of the losers, whether intact or torn apart, might have been those of niggers. So he ran. He ran to hide in the root cellar of the place he had called his home.

He carefully refolded the letter and returned it to a small pocket he had sown inside his saddlebag almost ten years ago. He had kept the child to spite her. There had been two: a boy and a girl. The boy died about one hour after it was born. He watched it die. It was blue and it wouldn't stop crying, and then it just died. He buried them both with his own hands. He didn't mark the graves because he knew he would never see that place again.

Keeping the girl proved that he was not the low creature that she had said he was. It proved her a liar. Lying was a sin. He hoped she burned in hell for it. He carted the infant in a buckboard from place to place, taking work as hired help. At first he fed it goat's milk from a spoon. Then a woman told him about soluble food and all he had to do was mix it with milk and feed the baby using an India Rubber Nipple on a bottle. He ordered it all special. He was good to her.

As he had been asked, he named her Theodosia, but he never called her that. He called her "girl." Once she got old enough to coo and smile, he grew almost fond of her. He looked forward to coming home to find her in the crib where he'd left her. He liked picking her up to stop her crying. He learned to camp near enough to people so that women heard the baby's bawling. They invariably offered to look after her when he worked bucking hay, or plowing or hammering rails.

All said she looked like an angel; and after countless such testaments, he saw her anew. Her downy blonde hair became a sign of blessedness, her white skin as clean as rain and rich as heavy cream, eyes so big and blue they seemed destined to see not just the sky, but the heavens beyond. The dead child was the price to pay for this one. In the Bible, God's gifts carried a price. His dead wife had cursed him, but God had other plans. He was not cursed. His wife's deathbed rants did not have to be his fate. He had, for the first time in years, some hope. So he devised a plan, and he had to bring it to fruition before the girl could read. As a lone man with a baby, he got all kinds of sympathy. Folks were always ready to give him work. All he had to do, he figured, was to find the right spot and settle in. He would make something of himself. Then, when he showed the girl the letter, she would not recognize the man so bitterly described as the righteous, caring father before her. Those vicious words would mean nothing to her because the man they cursed was dead.

4

"It may be well here to remark that with all beings there must be much fortuitous destruction... For instance a vast number of eggs or seeds are annually devoured, and these could be modified through natural selection only if they varied in some manner which protected them from their enemies. Yet many of these eggs or seeds would perhaps, if not destroyed, have yielded individuals better adapted to their conditions of life than any of [those] which happened to survive.

- Charles Darwin
"The Origin of Species"

Theodosia's dirty, still-bare feet swung freely as the afternoon train rattled toward Fort Smith. The plump, matronly woman sitting next to her had run a damp cloth across her face, erasing some of the blood, but the bruises grew more impressive by the mile. The matron regularly placed a gentle hand on her legs to remind her not to swing them in that unladylike manner, a habit doubtless acquired while growing up practically wild in the Indian Territories without a woman's guiding hand.

There was little to see out the windows, so Theodosia inspected the heads of the two Marshals sitting in front of her. One of them was bald. She imagined hand-drawn faces on the pale, white skin perfectly framed by an iris of sandy-colored hair... Eyes, nose, great big, bushy eyebrows. She giggled at the comic image, so lifelike before her.

The matron smiled down at her. 'A sweet enough girl,' she thought. 'So pretty - even with all the blood and bruises.' It was hard to believe what they said about her. Those ravishers must have corrupted her, or lied. In the old days she had heard about Indians stealing white women and bewitching them so completely that they didn't want to leave. Those poor women weren't to blame. Nor was this child. When the woman's husband died five years ago, she sold most of his land and rented what she could not sell (because though he possessed this land, he, as a white man, could not legally own land in Indian Territory and like everyone else just leased it awaiting the inevitable day when it would cease to be Indian land and become theirs). With the proceeds she opened a boarding house. It specialized in near-wayward women, who, under her supervision, did laundry and sewing to pay their keep. She was known throughout the town for good works. She was the rational choice to accompany this girl to Fort Smith, and comfort her throughout the recitation of her undoubtedly humiliating near-enslavement and probable ravishment at the hands of those colored fiends.

Sitting next to the earnest, imposing woman who occasionally turned to smile sweetly at her, Theodosia giggled, still amused by the imaginary face on the bald man's head. The woman and the Marshals turned at the incongruous laughter. The woman pursed her lips in disapproval because the moment warranted solemnity; men were dead; a girl violated; justice to be done. Theodosia shut her lips tight and buried her chin in her neck to muffle the sounds.

Gaping out the window, she wondered if she had walked this terrain. She usually walked behind her father's wagon instead of riding in it. She got to see things that way. Walking, she could chase a butterfly, or scurry off the road to see what the buzzards pecked at. The first time she ran at them, one big bird in particular stood its ground, flapping its huge black wings threateningly. She stood hers, too. Fascinated by its ugliness, she moved closer. Its blood-spotted beak protruded from a naked, wrinkled head. Next to it sat a ravaged carcass. Skunk stink sharpened the air. The big bird looked like a devil. She smiled as she circled it, watching its eyes follow her. It did not give an inch. She wanted it. She wanted its wings and its protection. She wanted the look in its eyes. She envied the fear she knew it must evoke in most—the disgust at its repellant face. She saw herself in it. Another wild thing. She screamed and charged like a bull. Startled, it flapped its big wings impossibly slowly, with a strange combination of frenzy and laziness—so slowly you couldn't imagine them wafting the big, black body off the ground. Then, surprisingly, haltingly, it took to the sky.

Her father never looked back for her. After wandering, she always ran back to take her place beside the wagon. If she got tired, she'd jump on the back. He rarely knew she'd been gone. They rarely spoke. There was nothing to say. She didn't care where they were going, and she didn't care about him. She followed because there was nothing else to do. She liked to watch him, though. He was like another of the animals she spied on. She watched his beard grow after he shaved. She'd seen men with full, lush beards and marveled at the wispy spottiness of his. She observed how the dirt and grime settled in the creases on his face, like fine black chalk lines. She gawked on the rare occasions he'd emerge from a saloon having bathed and shaved, no longer her father; no longer the silent creature of the plains, the foothills, the road and the wagon, no longer the embodiment of the dust they raised and the mud they trod. At those times, he emerged a man. She'd regard him with a mix of pride and fear. That he could present as a man meant that she might be more than just the spawn of the earth, more than a ghostly thing treading this particularly verdant purgatory. It might also mean that he was simply more—better than her and the life they led, underneath it all—and as such, would one day realize it and leave her behind. She felt relief as the sharp smell of sweat crept back on him, as the spotty beard dotted his face, as the dirt besmirched him once again. Only then could she relax and heedlessly skip behind the wagon as he moved from place to place, without fear of his recognizing her worthlessness and discarding her for it—for it was his as well.

When he went off to work, she wandered various towns and watched the passersby. A filthy waif in shabby clothes and tattered shoes, she imagined herself invisible. Many stared and she never knew why, so she ignored them. She watched them with the same fascination with which she watched the vultures; walking in and out of shops, climbing in and out of buggies, pouring out of smoke-drenched railcars, their habits were no less strange to her. How this one wore his vest too tight... the woman's mincing steps as she eyed the ground and scurried as if pursued... any rich man's swagger... She studied them all. To what end she never even considered.

~ ~ ~

In Muskogee, the hordes had thundered and raged. At the Fort Smith station, the much smaller crowd gaped at the steaming train in silence. They knew that living, breathing ghosts would step off that train. Judge Parker would sentence them to hang. There might be delays; there might be reversals, but they would hang, and die. They were more than outlaws now. They were every man and woman's fate. They were dead men.

The guards surrounding Rufus looked out the windows as the train slowed. When they saw armed Marshals push their way through the crowd, they herded their shackled prisoners out of their seats. The silence held as the Bucks emerged, a silence amplified by the wordless rustle and shuffle of bodies shifting, shoes creaking as they raised their owners to maximum height. The Marshals took positions before and behind the Bucks, and marched them forward three blocks to the government barracks that held the Ft. Smith jail. The crowd followed respectfully behind, and stopped en masse as the massive wooden doors opened to receive the notorious outlaws. The crowd stood still as the gates shut before them, blotting the dead men from view.

This was the second time Rufus Buck had walked through those gates.

~

"Rufus Buck. Introducing whiskey into Indian Territory," called the bailiff of Judge Parker's court.

"His plea?" Parker asked the defense counsel as he rifled his notes to ratify the name of the accused. Yes. He recognized that name.

"Not guilty, your honor," replied the lawyer.

Parker read his notes in silence for what seemed a very long time. "There is a witness? One of my Deputy Marshals. John

Garrett?"

The Negro Garrett stood in the gallery and then sat down again.

"He still owes me money for that liquor," Rufus yelled to the gallery's titters.

Parker stared at the boy. The painful interview with John Buck and the Chief of the Euchee Creeks still stung—an interview that had made manifest his growing impotence and coming obsolescence.

Parker scanned the crowd. "Is your father in this courtroom?" he asked.

Rufus shrugged, but did not turn to look. He hoped that his father was not there. He hoped that he was. All heads swept the room, but no one came forward. Among a few men standing at the back, Parker saw one turn toward the door. Parker watched him leave. It was John Buck.

Parker shook his white, whiskered head in sadness. At moments like these he cherished the good his office could do. He sat even more erect on his imposing throne, filled with pride at the work he would do here today.

He glared at the defense. "You are asking the jury to take the word of this..." Parker rifled his notes, "...this 17 year-old boy against that of a duly recognized Marshal?"

Marshal Garrett smiled at that. It meant the Judge had made up his mind. There would be no discussion of the crime, no evidence, no testimony—and if forced Garrett would have had to admit—very little justice. But that suited Garrett fine. It meant no one would learn the truth of it.

The defense attorney, acknowledging his case lost, hung his head, not even attempting to answer Parker's wholly rhetorical question. However, in doing so, in failing to answer, the defense attorney gained Parker's respect. Some new arrivals with their eastern ways and Supreme Court ideas defended any idiocy, coddled any lie without the slightest nod to justice. At least this one had the benefit of shame, Parker thought. His case made, his dispensation of justice unchallenged, Parker sat erect in his grand chair, behind his ornate desk and spoke directly to the jury with every ounce of command he could muster.

"It is inconceivable," he said, "that a jury of honest men would take the word of this boy over that of a Marshal who daily risks his life for meager reward to maintain law and order in these Territories. Therefore, I will not even attempt to instruct you on how to reach your verdict. That is foregone. I will tell you why your act could be the salvation of this young man, so young, but already on a road to petty criminality or outright perdition. He is proof of the fact that the toleration of lawlessness breeds more of the same."

Parker surveyed the object of his judgment. "He is the son of our crimes, the spawn of the injustice and incivility we tolerate."

Buck stopped fiddling with a piece of string dangling from his sleeve as the drone of Parker's voice, so much like Callahan's, ceased. He looked up at the bench and saw the old man staring meaningfully down at him, as if he wanted something from him. Rufus shrugged, dismissive and questioning, wondering why he stared like that. He literally heard nothing more until the Judge said, "...return once you have reached your inevitably just verdict and sentence, up to the maximum of 90 days in the Ft. Smith jail. That might provide sufficient time for him to ruminate on the course his life might take, on whether he, knowledgeable of Christian ways, will tread God's path, or continue a journey that leads to lawlessness and damnation."

Rufus guarded a smile. Judge Isaac Parker had condemned the great outlaw Cherokee Bill to death. Bill sat on Murderer's Row on the first floor of the Ft. Smith jail; and the same Judge had now condemned him—Rufus Buck—to that same jail. Rufus could have danced and jerked like the woman in the Freedman church. It took everything he had to hide the glee tugging at the sides of his mouth. He was going where bloodstained black angels dwelt—larger and grander than ordinary men, so much larger than this judge and his jury, the fools who thought they punished him but had no idea that they fulfilled a dream so big it smacked of destiny—bloodstained black angels; and Rufus would walk among them. Bells should have tolled... Choirs sung...

~ ~ ~

The Fort Smith jail smelled of unwashed men and their piss, shit, liquor and vomit. Marshals marched Rufus upstairs to the third floor, which housed the whiskey peddlers, the petty thieves, and anyone with a sentence of less than one year. He counted the cells he passed—twelve in all. He saw another prisoner turn at the end of the hall, so he imagined there were more cells on the other side. The floor below, he figured, would be exactly the same, except he knew it held the thieves and robbers. And the first floor housed Murderer's Row; just a few feet below him... Cherokee Bill.

He continued down the boisterous corridor, awed at the brown and yellow streaks dripping down the walls as if they had, in some pitiable past, wept dirty tears. He had never chewed tobacco, but seeing the squirt like so much madly spattered paint, he figured he'd have to take it up. In their cells, men insistently scratched their heads and privates in tribute to the omnipresent lice. Flies attacked the shit buckets in the corner of each cell.

"How do you get to the first floor," he asked his guards.

"Kill somebody," the guard replied and doubled up laughing.

Rufus regarded the laughing man with a pallbearer's mien.

Part II

Luckey Davis was a short, coal black Negro; Lewis Davis a light-skinned Indian half a year younger but half a foot taller. Random children roamed the streets of Okmulgee, colliding off of one other like marbles. They met, teamed up for this or that mischief, and went their separate ways. Lewis and Luckey, on the other hand, met when they were fourteen, each an only child, and despite their differences—one black, one tall, one short, one Creek—they stuck.

They both knew it had something to do with their names. It was a permanent source of wonder. They would stare at each other and just grin with the outrageousness of it. Their meeting had to be more than coincidence. Both alone. Both "Davis..." And soon, their friendship exuded an import befitting its downright preternatural inspirations. They drifted from their respective homes and grew to rely on each other. "Home" became where they mutually laid their heads.

"So we brothers, right?" Lewis said, stirring a fire as they sat, soon to sleep beneath a star-gilt sky.

"The Davis brothers," Luckey replied, his white teeth contrasting black skin in a rare smile.

Their bond instilled courage that neither knew he had. With

the other behind him, each could be a bigger man. Lewis loved horses and Luckey wanted to drive a train. Unable to decide between the two, they settled on owning a farm. They would graze cattle and raise crops—on land smack in the railway's path. They'd lease the land to the railroad at exorbitant rates with the caveat that Luckey got to drive a train. Dreams cost, so they took to thievery. They stole food to eat or anything else they could grab risk free. They stole 20 scrawny hogs from the small George ranch near Tulsey Town. The idea was to fatten them up and sell them good and plump.

"They ain't getting' any fatter," Luckey said after one week. The hogs had grazed down to nothing the small patch the boys had fenced off. They thought about moving the fence so the hogs could get some fresher grass, but the fence wood was so spindly and the whole so flimsy that Lewis said that there wouldn't be "enough o' nothin' left to keep nothin' inside." They sat to ponder the problem and decided to sell the hogs right away. Using their hats, they herded the 20 hogs through Tulsey Town to Olcutt's store. The old proprietor looked askance at the Negro and the Creek with an unusual wealth of hogs.

"Where'd you get 'em?" he asked.

"We raised 'em out in the woods," Lewis said.

"From pups," Luckey added. Lewis kicked him.

Mr. Olcutt was not above larceny of his own. He offered the boys $21 for the hogs. Before their protestations grew too loud, he said he'd make up another $40 in store merchandise.

The boys did some counting on their fingers and grudgingly accepted the deal. Both immediately scanned store shelves from top to bottom to identify the items they'd take. Both stopped at the same spot—a shelf of Hostetter's Bitters. Promoted for the cure of "dyspepsia's pangs that rack and grind the body and depress the mind; slow constitutional decay that brings death nearer day by day...," the substance was spiked with bitters to give it medicinal airs but remained 47% alcohol. The boys took all the Hostetters they could carry, not realizing or not caring that it was worth only $12. Olcutt gave them each a sack to put it in. They scrambled back to the woods where they drank themselves insensible.

Unfortunately for Mr. Olcutt, the hogs' rightful owners arrived at his store, recognized their livestock and marched it away. However, Olcutt knew providence was with him when a good citizen brought in a cartridge belt he had found in the woods. Olcutt immediately recognized it. Reaching into an inside compartment, he pulled forth the same $21 he had given to Lewis and Luckey. To Olcutt, it was a fine days' work. He sold $12 worth of Hostetter's for $21.

When the boys ran out of bitters and sobered up, they realized that they had nothing left but aching heads. They looked at each other. Grins split both their faces. That's when they decided to traffic in liquor.

That's when they met Rufus Buck.

~

Rufus watched like a bored referee as Maoma July, a full-blooded Creek just a little younger than he—all bones and angles from head to toe—frenetically kicked a bleeding white man who lay on the ground in a self-protective huddle. Maoma's sidekick, Sam Sampson, a slow-witted Creek teen, injected an occasional boot of his own, but mainly encouraged with head thrusts and fist pumps. Spotting the melee, Lewis and Luckey hid behind some barrels and watched, both sensing the scene to be profoundly instructional.

"You owe us the money," Rufus insisted in a reasonable tone. "You know you do 'cause you drank the liquor."

At "liquor," Lewis and Luckey's were hooked.

"I ain't got it, you goddam thievin' nigger."

Maoma's boot met the white man's head several more times.

"I know you ain't got it," Rufus rationally explained. "If you had it, Maoma wouldn't be kickin' you, 'cause I woulda taken it. You gotta get it. You got to give it to us."

Throughout most of this speech, Moama kicked with such frantic speed and increasing fury that he risked both comedy and his own exhaustion.

"Okay. I know. I know."

"Hold on Maoma," Rufus said, but the boy continued his mad, lightning-fast kicking.

"Maoma!" Rufus yelled. "Hold on."

Maoma stopped, panting furiously and licking his lips. The man was an Okmulgee drunk known for his predilection for young Indian girls and his loud ridicule of Indian men for the amusement of other whites. The drunk pulled his hands from his face.

"I'll get your goddamned money." He spat blood on the ground.

"How you gonna get it?" Rufus asked.

"I'm gonna steal it. How you think I'm gonna get it?"

"Who from?"

He looked at Rufus quizzically. "I ain't gonna tell you."

"Kick him some more."

"From Pinch's. The boarding house. I heard her boarders say she keeps money in there."

Rufus had asked in case he could rob the place himself before the drunk got to it. But Pinch's was a white woman's house smack in the middle of town. He couldn't rob it without making a big commotion and getting every law in Okmulgee after him.

"Okay. Tomorrow, right here, same time, you bring what you owe, or," Rufus paused and straightened his back to the point of tipping backwards, "... or be gone from the Territory," he intoned.

The drunk wobbled to his feet, spat again, and with a hand to his battered head, stumbled from the alley.

"Be gone, you hear me!?" Rufus hollered after him, reveling in the Biblicality of it, the stentorian authority.

As the drunk passed, Lewis and Luckey revealed themselves and watched him retreat. Both their faces bright lanterns of admiration, they turned in unison to Rufus, Maoma and Sam. Rufus stood a little taller as they walked eagerly, yet warily toward him.

Ever the loyal Lieutenant, Maoma took his place at Rufus' side, thrilled that these newcomers had seen him in his glory—giving a white man the tip of his boot. Slow-witted Sam stood a dutiful half step behind.

Luckey and Lewis stopped a few feet from the trio. Nobody spoke. Lewis, towering over all of them, nodded his head slightly in a greeting that could have been mistaken for a twitch.

"Whatchu want, then?" Maoma finally demanded.

"I'm Lewis and this is my brother Luckey."

Sam's brow knitted.

"He's your brother?" Rufus asked.

"Uh huh," they replied in unison.

"You don't look nothin' like brothers.

"We is," said Luckey.

"Like real brothers?" Maoma asked.

"Yep," Lewis replied.

"You got different Mas or Daddys or somethin'?" Rufus asked.

"Both," said Lewis.

"Then you ain't goddamn brothers." Maoma insisted. "You ain't nothin'."

"Is to!" Lewis growled.

"You ain't nothing," Moama mocked.

Lewis took a threatening step forward. Maoma matched it.

All heard the hammer cock. Luckey had pulled a Colt revolver and straight-armed his gun at Maoma's head.

"Take it back," Luckey demanded.

Maoma stared down the barrel and at Luckey's dogged black face. "I take it back," Maoma said dejectedly. "You're goddamn twins if you want," he muttered as he took his place behind Rufus.

Lewis and Luckey smiled at each other. Luckey uncocked his gun and placed it back in his belt. Rufus rushed toward him.

"Lemme see," as he reached for the weapon. Luckey proudly handed it over. Rufus felt its heft, checked the bullets in the chamber, closed one eye and aimed down his arm at passersby who momentarily filled the narrow gap between the two buildings.

"Where'd you get it?" Rufus asked.

"He stole it," Lewis replied. "Off a dead man."

"If he was dead you didn't stole it," Maoma said.

"Can I see it?" Sam asked as he joined the assembly. Rufus handed it to him. He had time to grin foolishly before Maoma snatched it from him.

"We gotta get guns," Rufus said, almost to himself. "You just ain't outlaws without guns."

~

To commemorate the capture of the notorious Rufus Buck gang—for bringing to heel the territory's most sadistic rapists and murderers—Parker's clerk, Virgil Purefoy, innocently presented the Judge with a bound copy of a book entitled *The Origin of Species* by Charles Darwin. He did not know that his gift might have been venom for all of the anguish it would reap. Having planned it as a birthday gift, Virgil had taken great care with its selection, and had ordered it all the way from New York City. The capture of the Bucks seemed as auspicious an occasion as any for the presentation.

"It was the talk of cultured people everywhere," Virgil told Parker. "At least that's what I hear from friends in the East. I haven't read it myself, but I knew it would be fitting for a man of your education and reputation."

The gesture touched Parker. "What is its subject?" he asked as he thumbed the introduction.

Purefoy knitted his brow. "I have heard that it tells how creatures become what they are—over time... birds and beasts, over hundreds or thousands of years. Some say that maybe even humans... how we've grown from lower things..."

That made no sense to Parker, but he smiled appreciatively nonetheless.

A sudden commotion sounded outside the door. Purefoy left to investigate. Parker read a bit of the page to which he had thumbed.

> *After remarking that negroes and mulattoes enjoy an immunity from certain tropical diseases, he observes, firstly, that all animals tend to vary in some degree, and, secondly, that agriculturists improve their domesticated animals by selection; and then, he adds, but what is done in this latter case "by art, seems to be done with equal efficacy, though more slowly, by nature, in the formation of varieties of mankind, fitted for the country which they inhabit."*

Virgil returned with Deputy N.B. Irwin and Marshal Samuel Haynes. They greeted the Judge and reported that the Buck gang had been safely delivered to the Ft. Smith jail. They had even apprehended Lewis Davis, the fifth gang member, a Creek Indian who had gone missing after the fire fight. Mindful of Purefoy's watchful eye and tender feelings, the Judge placed his new volume carefully on his desk as he listened.

A middle-aged woman barged into the room half-dragging a dirty girl.

"She must be seen to immediately!" the woman insisted. "You can see the state she's in. You can imagine what she's endured..."

"This is Mrs. Pinch," the Deputy said. "She chaperoned the girl here from Muskogee."

"Who is she?" asked Parker, eying the girl.

The Marshal coaxed the Parker to a discreet corner.

"She must be seen to immediately!" Mrs. Pinch again demanded.

"This was the girl with the Buck gang," Irwin whispered.

Parker ogled the child.

"She wasn't a victim?"

"We're not sure. No one's talked to her. Thought you might be the one to do it, sir."

Parker hadn't taken his eyes off the girl. She stared back like a wolf.

"Leave her here with me," Parker replied.

Irwin and Haynes herded the protesting Mrs. Pinch from the room. The door shut. Parker and the girl each took a moment to absorb the sudden silence. When it grew heavy, Parker moved slowly and deliberately to his desk. Theodosia watched him. Just as slowly and deliberately, he picked up the glass pitcher and poured himself some water. She watched. At first, he didn't realize that he was moving as if he'd been left with a bobcat instead of a girl.

"What's your name?" he finally asked, forcing himself to behave naturally.

Words broke her blinkless stare. Her attention darted around the room like that of any child.

"Theodosia."

"Where are your mother and father?"

"My mother's dead. I don't know where my daddy is."

"How did you get so bruised up?"

"My Daddy beat me."

"Why did he do that? Were you bad?"

She giggled. "Yes." She giggled some more. "I was very, very bad."

2

After one week of his 90-day sentence, Rufus had settled into the dull, dirty prison routine. He slept. He ate when they brought him food. Since the guards snuck liquor to the inmates who could pay, half the prisoners were drunk at any given time. Most days, the third floor guards opened the cell doors to minimize fights and provide somewhat less fetid air; inmates freely wandered the halls. But what Rufus most wanted—travel between floors—was forbidden. After a while, though, he noticed that some prisoners did climb up and down those all-important stairs at will. These were the prisoners who fetched and carried for the guards, brought food and hauled the waste buckets outside.

"How come they get to do that?" he asked his cell mate, a middle-aged thief named Otis Wiggins.

"They're Trustees," he replied. "They pass slop... haul shit."

"How'd they get that?"

Wiggins smiled knowingly. He'd heard it before. "Ain't gonna happen. They don't escape. None of 'em do so you can forget about it."

"I ain't goin' nowhere," Rufus replied, "'cept the first floor."

"You gonna kill somebody?" Wiggins laughed and slapped

his knee in mirth.

"How do you get to be a Trustee?" Rufus repeated.

"You got any money?"

"No."

"What you want so bad on the first floor? And what you offerin' for tellin' you how to get there?"

At first Rufus didn't want to say it out loud. A Destiny was a sacred thing to be closely guarded. But then his pride kicked it.

"I got somethin' for Cherokee Bill," he boasted. He grandly turned his back on his cell mate, imagining his respectful envy. At the sound of dismissive laughter, he wheeled around.

"Bill don't want shit from nobody. 'Cept a set o' wings to fly his black ass outta here," the cell mate said.

Rufus turned back to face the empty hallway. "How you get Trustee?" he repeated as if Wiggins hadn't spoken.

Wiggins swigged from his bottle. "You crazy, ain't you?" he asked.

"How you get to be a Trustee!?" Rufus demanded.

Amused at this doggedness Wiggins answered. "Kiss guard's ass," he said.

And Rufus did. He became a model prisoner. He smiled at the guards and thanked them for every action on his behalf, no matter how minor or mandatory. He played the innocent. He walked with a teen's jaunt instead of a man's swagger and beamed youthful innocence like a beacon. Otis shook his head in disbelieving admiration at the breadth of his performance.

"Boy, I seen some ass kissin' in my time, but this is what they call a symphony. You want somethin' awful bad, don't you?"

"Me an' Bill gonna change everything," Rufus declared.

"Well whoo hoo for you," Otis smirked. "Ain't you one big, important man."

Rufus beamed with sincere gratitude at the compliment; he considered it a statement of fact, really. The childish innocence of it swept Wiggins' breath away. This was the strangest boy he had ever seen.

As the weeks passed, Rufus spied an opportunity. As one of the thinner, more dissolute Trustees swept the floor, Rufus rushed at him, slammed him to the wall and grabbed at his broom. Rufus expected a quick victory, but the wiry old man held onto that broom like it was salvation. Rufus gritted his teeth and yanked for all he was worth, almost swinging that old man like a puppy at the end of a rope, all to the staccato accompaniment of stifled grunts and squeals. Finally, breathlessly, Rufus freed the broom as the old man crashed to the floor.

"Now you jus' keep your mouth shut, old man." Rufus straightened himself up and started sweeping the hall as if nothing had happened. "You be nice to the guards and they might give you another broom," he helpfully said at the man on the floor as he swept.

No one questioned why he was sweeping. The guards assumed he was supposed to and they subsequently assumed that he should do other things, too, like empty shitters, or run liquor. Rufus became a self-appointed Trustee. Eventually, someone noticed that his name was missing from the official rolls and this omission was immediately corrected.

Before long, Rufus extended his skills to the second floor, which housed thieves and brutes whose crimes stopped short of murder or rape. Here again, he became beloved of the guards and a disconcerting curiosity to the inmates. To score points with guards, he ratted on anyone for any infraction. Prisoners soon learned that if a guard warned against drinking and fighting, the next drink had better be out of Rufus' sight. His bald-faced snitching evoked amazement. How dumb must this boy be, they thought? Rufus, however, simply sought the shortest distance to his goal. Snitching made him especially beloved of the most influential guards, so he did as much of it as possible.

"Boy, someone gonna stick a knife in you sure as you breathe," Otis Wiggins told him after his reputation as informant grew notorious. "Folks up here might be whisky runners and pickpockets, but second floor got some hard cases will surely break you up in pieces."

This had not occurred to Rufus. They were in jail. Guards were everywhere. It seemed irrational to him that in a house of correction he should fear doing the right thing, even though he did it for all the wrong reasons. After his roommate's alarming speech, however, he noticed the looks on some of his victim's faces. He then took to carrying a six-inch truncheon fashioned from a mop handle artfully split, with a dense rock wedged and strung into its end.

"Look like the Injun got himself a tomahawk," Wiggins scoffed, drunk, as he hopped unsteadily from one foot to the other chanting "woo woo woo woo" and beating his lips with an open palm.

Looking at the stunted weapon, Rufus sprouted another of his ear-to-ear grins and completely ignored Otis' drunken flailing. It was natural and noteworthy, he thought, that the idea for this weapon had suddenly come to him. He considered this—the automatic creation of an authentic Indian artifact—yet another sign from On High that his cause was just and his direction true. As his cell mate stumbled to the floor, giggling through his "woo woos," Rufus sat on the bed and proudly considered his creation.

He used it only once. There were no preliminaries to the attack. As forewarned prisoners watched from inside and outside their cells, a thick brute of a second-floor inmate waited. When Rufus passed, he wrapped his thick arm around the boy's neck.

"You like to talk, do you niggerinjun? Talk now."

Unable to breath, Rufus didn't make a sound. He reached into his pocket and pulled the truncheon. Inmates either shook their heads from side to side in disappointment or up and down in anticipatory approval. Rufus swung the truncheon wide and brought it down on the brute's knee. The big man swallowed a scream and fell to the ground. Free, Rufus felt his neck as if to make sure it was still there, and then turned his attention to the man on the ground. He stared at him as if shocked and betrayed by such behavior. He then brought the truncheon down on his head. Blood spilled down the man's face.

"What'd you wanna go do that for?" Rufus asked in all sincerity, and then hit him again with the truncheon. Seeing the blow coming, the man turned in time to take it on the back. He fell to his knees but struck out and grabbed Rufus's ankle. As if swatting a large, persistent fly Rufus swung the truncheon down again and again and again until only breathing moved the big body lying on the ground. Rufus perplexedly eyed the inmates watching, as if to ask why he was forced to face such injustice and inconvenience. As he did, they slowly turned their attentions elsewhere.

With no guards in sight, Rufus grabbed the big man's hands and dragged him toward the steep steps. The other inmates watched, rapt as if seeing a particularly unpredictable animal go about its business. At the top of the stairs, Rufus sat on the ground, pressed his feet against the body's mass, and kicked at it. Inch by inch, the body slid across the first step. One final kick and it went tumbling down, hitting the bottom with a decisive thump. The guards came running and by the time they got there, Rufus was trotting down the steps. The inmates rushed en masse to the top to see the rest of the show. Rufus stared down at the body with impassive curiosity and proceeded to tell the guards most of the truth. He failed to mention the weapon—the only lie, and that by omission. The audience opened their mouths and almost imperceptibly nodded their heads in appreciation as they disbursed, amid mumbles, to their various posts on the second floor. Soon, multiple versions of the event swirled around the prison. Rufus Buck had earned himself a reputation.

~

After Rufus Buck's trial and removal to the Ft. Smith jail for a 90-day sentence, Marshal John Garrett stood from his seat and nodded to a few of the men and jurors as they left the courtroom. He shook a congratulatory hand or two as he made his way toward the judge who stood at his desk accepting compliments from a coterie of respectable townspeople.

"I just wanna thank you, Judge," Garrett mumbled, head

low to telegraph humility. "It was mighty Christian of you to stand up for me like that."

"I would have done no less for any of my Marshals," Judge Parker proclaimed. "I just hope that I'm able to do a service for that young man."

"'I sure hope so too, Judge," Garrett replied. "He wouldn't be the first man you put on the righteous path." Garrett sincerely hoped that Rufus Buck would rot in hell. From his authority as a Marshal, Garrett made his place in the world and the money in his pocket. He would let no white man challenge it. He'd be damned if he'd let a half-breed Creek do so. As he watched the Judge leave, Garrett shoved a pinch of tobacco in his lip. He chewed a while and spat the juice on the courthouse floor.

John Garrett's trials with Rufus Buck began indirectly—when Luckey Davis approached him with a dream of selling liquor. Garrett knew Luckey from the Negro Freedmen town.

"How you gonna sell liquor?" Garrett asked him.

"I don't know," Luckey replied, his tall, moon-faced Indian friend looking on like a hungry pup. "That's what I'm askin' you for."

"I don't sell no liquor boy," Garrett knocked Luckey's hat off. "And you go tellin' anyone that I do and I will shoot you stone dead." Garrett looked at Lewis. "And him, too." Lewis took a step backwards. Garrett scrutinized both, shifting the tobacco plug from one cheek to the other. He was a big man, and a Marshal. He could kill without excuses. It was known that he had done so.

Neither boy dared moved. They knew they were being studied.

"Go see my brother Joshua," Garrett finally mumbled.

Lewis and Luckey stood frozen as Garrett walked away. "I know where Joshua lives," Luckey sputtered once Garrett was out of earshot. Despite his fear, Lewis nodded softly.

Two days passed during which other tasks demanded the boys' attentions—like following that hawk or stealing supplies. Neither admitted to fearful procrastination. At night, after hearing Luckey's soft snores, Lewis practiced cradling his shot-up gut and miming a dying man's agonies—the fate he feared at the Garrett brothers' hands. Meanwhile, Lewis dreamed that he was taller and older, that he scared men like Garrett and didn't have to be afraid.

On the third day they walked to Marshalltown, where the Freedmen lived. Black faces gradually outnumbered the brown and white ones. Lewis felt big and awkward, like he took up too much room. Luckey felt less wary, but no less out-of-place. He had been born here and his family still lived here, but he had never belonged. He had always sensed a cowering here. It felt like a weight that everyone carried, but nobody mentioned. They were all scared. They huddled here like threatened cows, helpless if a deadlier animal came along. He did not want to live that weakly. It was a chain around them. That's why he'd left. It's why he'd joined up with Luckey to live on the lam. With Luckey, no one tied his hands and feet together so that he couldn't hurt himself—and then asked him to appreciate it, or not to notice.

They heard the resonant clanging of hammer on iron from Joshua Garrett's blacksmith shop. He sold the liquor to all of Marshalltown as well as supplying some of the more notorious whiskey runners in the Territory. Garrett ignored the boys as they approached. He continued heating red hot iron over a fire, dipping it in a bucket to smoke and sinister hissings.

"What you want?" he finally deigned to ask.

"Liquor," Luckey replied.

Bending over his forge, Garrett shot a smile. "I ain't no saloon," he said after looking them up and down. He brought his hammer down in smaller taps.

"We want lotsa liquor," Luckey corrected. "To sell."

"You got lotsa money to buy it?" Garrett asked.

Luckey looked quizzically at Lewis, who shrugged with equal dismay. Neither had thought of money.

"We could sell it for you," Luckey blurted. "Like salesmen. We'd do good," he added, excited at his quick thinking.

"Get outta here," Garrett muttered, no longer amused.

"We can do it," Luckey insisted. We done stuff like it. We stolen some pigs and cattle. We make our own way at it. Your brother told us to come."

Garrett pointed threateningly with hot orange iron. "Don't you lie to me, little nigger. My brother ain't that much a fool."

"I ain't lyin'," Luckey protested. "Tell him, Lewis."

Unable to speak for imagining hot iron cooking his flesh, Lewis nodded his head up and down.

Garrett slowly relaxed the iron and turned toward his forge. "Get out," he said.

Luckey considered further appeals, but the ferocious banging and flying red sparks warned him away. He looked to Lewis for guidance, who shrugged, admitting defeat and turned to leave. Luckey followed. They walked back to Tulsey in total silence. Luckey wondered what he might have done differently to convince the blacksmith that he was more than just another 'little nigger.' Lewis silently mouthed self-deprecations on his failure to utter so much as a useful sound in the blacksmith's shop.

Soon after, they found Rufus Buck. They stumbled on a vision in the alley—someone not much older than they who sold liquor and managed his clientele with such inspiring professional brutality. As with Lewis and Luckey's first meeting, as with their names, there was Destiny in it.

They soon told Rufus about their plan to sell liquor and make enough to buy a farm. They told him all about Joshua Garrett's liquor operation. It soon fell into place: Rufus would receive money from the recently beaten drunk, which he would use to buy liquor from Joshua Garrett. After some wrangling, it was agreed that all five boys would split the profits equally, though Rufus would be the undisputed leader. Eventually, they agreed, they would take over all the liquor sales in the Territory. All would fear them. None would disobey.

They would call themselves the Rufus Buck Gang.

~ ~ ~

Like a fretful suitor, Rufus skulked outside Cherokee Bill's cell on the first floor of the Fort Smith Jail. He would pass the cell as often as he dared, determined to keep his eyes forward and not stare like a child. But as if on its own, his head would whip to the side trying to glimpse Bill's person. Bill did not notice him. It didn't help that Rufus hid from him at every opportunity. He even waited until Bill left his cell to collect his shit bucket. When he did, however, instead of holding it at extreme arm's length to the extent of his ability like he did with all the others, he found himself peeking inside to see if Bill's was any different; if it was formally more perfect or aromatically distinct. At times, he could have sworn it was. As for the hiding, Bill's light was too bright, his grandness too ostentatious for Rufus to survive a slight from him. If Bill did not recognize him as kindred, Rufus would be lost. He would be nothing—little more than the image of his devastated father. All of his plans and all the redemption he owed that broken old man with no idea how to deliver... all would be aborted if Cherokee Bill rejected him. He dared not approach.

Dapper Henry Starr always stood as if shielded inside a pristine cocoon as he sauntered through Murderer's Row. He never hurried. Screaming matches, fist fights, shit throwing fury, none of it fazed him. However, if someone dared touch him, if a speck of that shit had soiled his clothes, you imagined an explosion of the rageful indignation that sustained his pose as a gentleman bandit. How it would express itself you did not know. It might be anything from lingering butchery to a single, definitive blow. It might be subtle, long-term torture ingeniously devised. You didn't know. You just knew it would come, and so you did not test him. You did not touch him, for it was obvious that his very self, was, to him, and he believed it should be to others, the most precious of things. To sully it was a capital crime, the murder of a child, the rape of little girl, the kind of crime for which men sat in this shit-stinking hole called Murderer's Row.

In his early twenties, Henry had been born in Indian Territory to Tom and Mary Starr. He was nephew to Sam Starr, the full-blooded Cherokee married to Myra Belle Starr, aka "Belle," the notorious outlaw. But Henry bristled when some suggested that criminality was "in his blood."

"I was a good boy," he insisted. One-quarter Cherokee, he blamed his lawless reputation squarely on white men and their unjust ways. His mother's second husband, a white man, threw him out of the house for no reason. While working on a ranch, he was arrested for driving a wagon full of whiskey. He swore to the deputies that he was simply driving, as instructed, with no idea of his cargo, but they arrested him anyway. Only sixteen, he was told by a white lawyer that he had no choice but to plead guilty and Judge Parker might go gentle on him. So he did, and got the maximum. He was sentenced to 90 days in jail. Once free, he took work on another ranch. All went well until Marshals came to arrest him for horse theft, a charge of which he was, he swore to the heavens, entirely innocent. Thrown back in jail at Fort Smith, a cousin made his bail. To his own mind guilty of nothing, he had been twice unjustly arrested and incarcerated. This was his Territory. He was Cherokee and it was his (although to unschooled eyes he looked just like a white man). He would not rot in a white man's jail for crimes that he did not commit and even if he had were not crimes because this was his Territory. He failed to show up for trial. He shot and wounded one of the posse hired to hunt him down. He then approached the injured man and put a bullet in his heart at point blank range.

The sharp-eyed Starr soon noticed a young man often loitering near Bill's cell, casting furtive glances inside. Day after day, Starr watched, amused. He finally stepped quietly behind Rufus as the boy stole glances toward where Bill was.

"I see you're familiar with the exploits of our friend Crawford Goldby," Starr whispered. Rufus' broom leapt from his hand and thwacked against the floor.

"I didn't mean to scare you," Starr apologized with ironic sincerity.

"I ain't scared," Rufus rebutted, collecting his broom.

"Bill is our most famous resident."

"I know all about him," Rufus said.

"Heard stories?"

"I read it," Rufus proudly professed. "Everything they wrote."

"A scholar..." Starr enthused, genuinely surprised. "You have unexpected facets, like a diamond. I stole one o' those once. It was in a bank safe. Prettiest thing. Hard as steel and looking delicate enough to shatter like glass." He regarded Rufus for a moment. "Like a dirty diamond."

With mild exasperation, Starr noticed that Rufus had stopped listening and was trying to eye Bill on the sly. Then he realized...

"You must be the one I heard about," he said. "Half Negro, half Creek. Kicked the shit outta some big sonofabitch on the second floor." Starr laughed aloud. "Many facets," he said.

Rufus continued furtively glancing. He paid Starr little attention.

"You want to meet him?" Starr asked. The boy's breath quickened. Now Starr had his full attention. Buck stared like a starving child at bread.

"I think we should wait a while." Starr spoke slowly, devising a plan. "Let me talk to Bill. Yeah, I know him. I'd call myself a friend—his only friend. I understand Bill. He trusts me."

"When?" Rufus asked.

"Just give me time. Let me talk to him. It'll be soon."

Rufus now stared openly into Bill's cell, as if praying to it and awaiting its response. Starr moved to mimic the boy's angle on the cell and all he could see were Bill's boots up against the wall.

"Why'd they make you a Trustee?" Starr asked.

"I don't know," Rufus shrugged. "They didn't at first. I just started doin' it."

"Why?"

"To meet Bill. To get to Murderer's Row."

"Ever consider killin' someone?" Starr smiled.

Rufus stared blankly at him. "Got nothin' against it I guess."

Starr examined the young, eager, full-to-bursting yet somehow impassive face. The boy was waiting for something. Waiting to come alive, seeking some charge, some strike of a match that would set him alight. Starr had never seen this bizarre combination of emptiness and pressure-to-the-breaking-point. It was simplicity as a mighty force. It intrigued him.

"Go on," Starr said. "Push your broom. I'll let you know when it's time."

"What you jawin' about out there?" a voice hollered from within the cell. Rufus stood up straighter. His mouth opened and his eyes brightened with anticipation. It had to be Bill.

"Go on," Starr insisted, giving the boy a little shove. "Get."

Rufus did not take his eyes off the cell as he backed reluctantly down the hall.

3

At long intervals of time, out of millions of individuals reared in the same country and fed on nearly the same food, deviations of structure so strongly pronounced as to deserve to be called monstrosities arise;"

- Charles Darwin
"The Origin of Species"

Judge Parker sat alone in his chambers, numbed. There was no other word to match his state. It was new to him. 'Shock' did not describe it. 'Revulsion' was closer but did not convey the fear. As he listened he had felt a rising in his gut, a dizzying inside that presaged nausea. What he saw before him spoke with the leg-kicking charm of a child describing picnics and romps in the wood, but instead she described murders and torture. She giggled at the pain inflicted. He wanted to touch her to convince himself that she was real. At first he chose not to believe. He questioned. He challenged. He denied. But with childish artlessness she shook her blonde head and repeated horror after horror with juvenile delight encased in a bruised beauty as if such monstrosities were a natural part of living. He literally felt chills as he sat imperceptibly shaking his bearded, white-haired head as if that small act of denial would make her and everything she represented disappear.

He had been sitting here for minutes now. His clerk had entered and been summarily dismissed with no grace. The girl had been returned to the care of her matronly overseer. Judge Parker sincerely wondered if Mrs. Pinch was safe, but oddly felt she was. It had been an opportunity. A rare one, and she had taken it. She had reveled and luxuriated in it. An opportunity of blood and violence—of viciousness. Round and round these thoughts swirled and he could not stop them. In a vain attempt, he grabbed that book of Virgil Purefoy's. He leafed through its pages, searching for something to divert his mind. Nothing seized him, so he stopped at a random page and began to read.

> *As natural selection acts solely by the preservation of profitable modifications, each new form will tend in a fully-stocked country to take the place of, and finally to exterminate, its own less improved parent-form and other less favoured forms with which it comes into competition. Thus extinction and natural selection go hand in hand. Hence, if we look at each species as descended from some unknown form, both the parent and all the transitional varieties will generally have been exterminated by the very process of the formation and perfection of the new form.*

At first he didn't understand, so he read the words again, and rarely had any so unbalanced to him. He knew it must be their quick succession upon his most appalling interview, but nonetheless, these few words were like the first dashes of a sketch. He recognized an outline, a form, and something in him knew that the ensuing shape would be of great consequence to him.

> *But it may be urged that when several closely-*

> *allied species inhabit the same territory, we surely ought to find... many transitional forms. Let us take a simple case: in travelling from north to south over a continent, we generally meet... with closely allied or representative species, evidently filling nearly the same place in the natural economy of the land. These representative species often meet and interlock; and as the one becomes rarer and rarer, the other becomes more and more frequent, till the one replaces the other... By my theory these allied species are descended from a common parent; and during the process of modification, each has become adapted to the conditions of life of its own region, and has supplanted and exterminated its original parent-form and all the transitional varieties between its past and present states.*

Could the girl be this new thing, she and her fellow travelers, the Bucks? Would their ways supersede his? If so, they were a transitional form toward what kind of abomination he could not even imagine.

He sat considering the unthinkable, and it was Virgil Purefoy's doing, his young clerk who gazed upon him as if at an antique in oils. Perhaps there was malevolence in him equal to that Theodosia only less overtly bloodthirsty. Maybe he, too, was of this new kind. Both of them were guides to godawful fates—she toward the details of why Rufus Buck would writhe at the end of a rope; Purefoy toward Parker's own death, spiritually crippled with the idea of an unthinkably Godless tomorrow. The words with which Virgil Purefoy had gifted him had, on the most inconsequential brush, warned that his pain would burrow much deeper than the sinew and the bone. Virgil Purefoy would idolatrously march him into hell.

Dreading, yet unable to stop himself, as if carrying out a sentence for crimes pronounced on him by God, he turned to the book and he began to read.

~ ~ ~

On advice from Lucky and Lewis Davis, Rufus took the money he had received from selling liquor a few bottles at a time to blacksmith Joshua Garrett. On receiving the money from Rufus, Garrett provided three cases of brown whiskey in plain bottles that had been mixed with creek water and seasoned with chiles, tobacco, and a touch of strychnine to give it a much-appreciated kick. Rufus, Maoma, Sam, Lewis and Luckey loaded the crates onto a cart borrowed from John Buck's farm and headed for Okmulgee with visions of riches to come. Luckey and Lewis took every step alongside the cart as one step closer to their dream. Maoma imagined himself the dandy—fine clothes, silver belt buckle and matching money clip, a ruffled, painted lady on his arm and not a man in the Territory to challenge him. For Rufus, this old horse and meager cart was the first conveyance on the beginning of a journey that would take him to extraordinary places. Sam, Maoma's shadow—he dreamt no dreams.

Rufus took a hearty stock of liquor and the promise of more to Okmulgee. Luckey and Lewis carted bottles north toward

Tulseytown and Sam and Maoma sold east toward Muskogee. Proceeds were returned to Rufus, and all sat apprehensively at the end of the next day as he counted out the profits, providing a small allowance to each (and a larger one for himself) as he laid the remainder aside for the next stock purchase.

When the group returned to Joshua Garrett's shop to double their order, the blacksmith realized he'd underestimated them.

"I'm gonna hafta charge you two dollars a bottle," Garrett told them.

"That's twice as much," Rufus complained.

"I know that, but you orderin' more."

"That don't make sense. Don't cost you more."

"No. Cost *you* more."

Rufus shook his head. "Uh uh. I ain't payin' it," Rufus insisted. "It ain't fair."

Garrett contemplated the boy for a while, then broke a smile. "You ain't too stupid. Gotta respect that. Awright. Same price. Six cases."

Garrett had never seen anyone hand over money with that big a grin on his face. One quarter of the way back to Okmulgee, Maoma danced beside the cart, boxing the air in triumph over his leader's negotiating skill.

"We showed him. He said, 'You ain't stupid, huh.' He the stupid one thinkin' we gonna pay twice the money for the same liquor. Not the Rufus Buck Gang." The lumbering Sam occasionally hopped and hooted a chorus, but the rest smilingly let Maoma shout their pride. It was more than enough.

Again they set up shop in Okmulgee, stretching out north and east. The liquor was moving and the money was flowing. Rufus even took a page out of Joshua Garrett's book and raised his price. Walking the Okmulgee streets, Deputy Marshal John Garrett stopped Rufus, who smiled conspiratorially.

"I guess I don't need to set you up with no liquor, him bein' your brother an' all," said Rufus.

"Come over here boy," Garrett ordered as he walked to a side street. Rufus followed.

"You owe me money," Garrett said.

"I already paid your brother."

"You ain't paid me for not arrestin' you."

"Your brother sold me the goddamned whiskey," Rufus yelled in outrage. Garrett slammed him up against a nearby wall. One big hand pressed on Rufus' chest, the other rifled his pockets, pulling bills and coins when he found them. Furious, Rufus lunged, knocking Garrett away and leaping on him like a cat to claw the cash back from his thieving hands. Equally infuriated, Garrett hurled him face-down on the ground and dropped his knee and all of his considerable weight on the boy's back as he handcuffed him.

"You're under arrest," he grinned as he yanked Rufus to his feet.

Rufus was taken to the jailhouse in Muskogee, where he expected trial before the Indian Court. Throughout the trip he shouted invectives at Deputy John Garrett, calling him a whiskey peddler and a thief, chiding his blacksmith brother for collusion and occasionally impugning their mother's virtue. At the jail house, surrounded by lawmen, he told his tale and shouted for justice until he was hoarse with it.

Rufus didn't know that Joshua Garrett sold liquor to most of the deputies of the Muskogee district. The lawmen paid him no mind.

Hearing of Rufus' arrest, Luckey and Lewis took the wagon to Muskogee while Maoma and Sam stole a horse to make the trip. They bribed a deputy to let them see Rufus who captivated them with the tale of his epic battle with Marshal Garrett (in which he almost prevailed) and the subsequent injustices he'd suffered since his arrest.

"We'll tell 'em what happened." Maoma insisted. "When they take you to the court, we'll say his own brother sol' us the liquor."

"You boys travelin' to Arkansas?" an eavesdropping deputy said, "'cause that's where they takin' him."

"What for?" Rufus asked.

"Trial. What else?"

"They got a court right here."

"Not for whiskey. Not no more. Send 'em all to Ft. Smith. That's where he goin' for trial," the deputy assured. "Judge Isaac Parker hisself gonna do the honors—an' he ain't so soft on whiskey."

The subsequent silence and long faces mirrored the shattering of all of their plans, schemes and dreams. Seeing the fear and trepidation in his men, Rufus drew them close and spoke in a whisper that the deputy couldn't hear.

"You all get ready while I'm gone," he told them. "We're gonna protect ourselves. No one's gonna take our money. Get yourself some guns and some horses and wait for me."

All four shook their heads in assent. Each barely met Rufus' gaze before marching solemnly from the jailhouse. Once they had left, Rufus considered the difference between the local trial and imprisonment and their Ft. Smith equivalents. He would have known the judges in Muskogee or they'd have known his Daddy. He didn't know a soul in Ft. Smith, but he kept hearing the words, "Fort Smith," and then "Judge Parker" crept in. "Smith" "Parker" and the realization expanded like a butterfly's new wings. He slammed both palms against the rickety bars and surprised himself with the violent din.

"Whatchu doin' in there," the deputy hollered.

Rufus didn't answer. He grabbed one fist in the other to keep them still. He knew what Ft. Smith meant. He remembered why the name was so almighty powerful. The knowledge settled on his heart like a Fatherly hand. He could not have wished for a more portentous sign.

Cherokee Bill was waiting to die at Ft. Smith.

~ ~ ~

"What you jawin' about out there?" Bill hollered, curious about Starr's mutterings outside his cell. At the lack of reply he yelled, "Talkin' how the white man done you wrong?" Bill didn't even open his eyes as he goaded Starr.

"An interesting young man of the Negro and Creek persuasion," Starr answered as he entered the cell. Starr thoughtlessly positioned himself on Bill's cot. He propped his head against the wall near Bill's stockinged feet and set his boots near Bill's head. Bill, eyes still closed, matter-of-factly flung the boots and the legs attached to them to the ground. After seeking a comfortable position without elevating his feet, Starr reluctantly sat upright. He pulled the makings of a cigarette from his vest pockets and began to roll.

"Why can't you chew it like everyone else."

Starr ignored him.

"Who was it you were preachin' at?"

"A fan of yours. He's read all about you."

"He reads?"

"Uh huh. Wants to meet you."

Bill chuckled.

"I think you should," Starr replied.

Bill knew that Starr made few moves without calculating their potential benefit—to himself. "What do you get outta me meetin' him?"

It was Starr's turn to laugh. "Bill, you make me sound downright selfish, and that ain't the case."

"Oh no not you," Bill mumbled.

A flash of hurt crossed Starr's face so quickly that only Bill would have noticed, had he been looking.

"Anyway," Starr recovered, "I don't know what for. He's a boy. Beat the shit outta some big fucker upstairs. Got Trustee just so he could come down here and moon at you. He wants somethin'. I don't know what. Don't know if he knows. But he don't seem stupid and sounds like he'd cut off an arm for Cherokee Bill. Might be useful." Starr drew heavily on his cigarette. "Got some Turkish to go in here... smooth." He stared appreciatively at the smoke rising from the lit tip.

"How's it chew?"

Henry scowled. "You will never be a gentleman, Bill."

"You just smell sweeter 'n me, Henry, that's all."

"Wet dogs smell sweeter 'n you, Bill." Both men laughed. Starr puffed on his cigarette. Bill closed his eyes.

"Parker sentenced me to die twice," Starr mused," and twice

the Supreme Court said I get to live. I'm waitin' on my third trial and the way I see it, Parker is hell bent to kill me. And Bill, I smell too good to hang."

"I got a month before I die," Bill said.

"You worry 'bout dyin?"

"I worry about not dyin.'"

Ever since the angelic visitation of his youth, Rufus had felt propelled to some uncharted place. The world that he saw around him, the world to which Callahan had tried to immerse him at the Wealaka Mission School, the world at which his mother quietly railed, they were not his worlds. He knew that. They were not his rightful home. There was another. He sensed it in the tales of outlaws, the wild miles they traveled and free lives they led. The men who owned the artifacts precious to his struck-dumb father had lived in such worlds. He knew that in his bones. It was his world. He just had to find it. After his talk with Henry Starr, Rufus felt enormous relief. He felt himself closer to someone whom, he imagined, had been there and who could show him the way.

When he next encountered Henry Starr, Rufus answered Starr's questions while struggling to hide the fact that he was scared. What if he gave a wrong answer and Bill refused to meet him? He swore to say as little as possible.

"Where're your Ma and Pa?"

"Near Tulseytown."

"Your Daddy Creek?"

Rufus shook his head in the affirmative.

"Lotsa white folks all around Tulseytown."

"My Ma says ain't nothing to do 'bout 'em."

"You know it's white folks landed me in jail for things I

never done."

Rufus looked quizzically at him. "Ain't you white?"

Starr's countenance turned mockingly dark. "You blind, boy?" Rufus shrunk back until Starr smiled. "My Uncle was the great Cherokee Sam Starr, who inspired Belle Starr."

"The Bandit Queen," Rufus beamed, reciting her dime story tag.

"Yep," Starr boasted. "That's who I am."

Rufus was floating in his boots to be talking with a relative of Belle Starr.

"I ain't no white man," Starr insisted. Rufus gaped in mute appreciation. It was the first time he had heard such a statement as a boast. From every previous mouth, Creek, Negro or white, being white had been regarded as a point of power and pride.

"You don't like white folks," Rufus stated.

Starr smiled. "Nobody likes white folks," he said. "White folks don't like white folks."

Gaining courage, Rufus asked, "Then how come they let so many in the Territory."

"How old are you, boy?"

"Seventeen."

"I was kiddin' about everyone not likin' 'em. White folks is awfully fond o' themselves. They think everything belongs to them that someone else won't kill 'em for takin.'"

"You killed any?"

"Ain't sittin' on Murderer's Row for violent knittin.'"

"They gonna hang you?" Starr looked around at the condemned men lounging and spitting against the backdrop of black bars. He inhaled their stink. He hadn't thought about dying that day.

"That's what they want."

Rufus shook his head. "It ain't right."

"White folks like killin' Indians."

"My Mama said they want what they want."

"Always listen to your Mama, son," he said absently, "unless she married a white drunk sonofabitch."

"No, sir. My Daddy's all Creek."

In the mindless prison routine, Starr sometimes let himself forget. 'They gonna hang you?' the boy had asked. It should have been impossible to forget—that they wanted to snuff him out, to squish him like a fly on glass, a splat of blood and wiped away. At that moment, he was glad he had killed that deputy. An act of preemptive revenge. He thought that he should have killed more, done more damage to warm flesh instead of cold cash. Right then, he regretted that he had not been born a killer. Were he more like Cherokee Bill, there would have been more right in old man Parker trying to kill him. As it stood, it was just another white man's malevolence, this time dolled up as justice.

He saw his scowl reflected in Rufus' face. "Ignore me, boy," Starr said. "Just musin'. How long you in here for?"

"A little over fifty more days. I got ninety for liquor."

"You know they plan to hang Bill, too."

"Not if I got something to say on it."

Starr smiled. "Then let's see what you got to say. Come 'round tomorrow and meet Bill."

Starr abruptly turned and left. He didn't want to see the unfettered elation on the boy's face. He didn't know why he felt guilty. Buck was getting what he wanted—even more... to serve Bill's interest. He'd achieve his dream and then some.

'If something happens… if he dies in the process, well…' Starr thought somewhat unconvincingly, 'at least he'll die happy.'

~

When Henry Starr walked Rufus into Bill's cell, the great man was pissing in his bucket. When finished, Bill turned, tucking himself back into his pants, shook some drops from his boot and walked toward Rufus. He stretched out his hand. Rufus sighed with relief at the great honor. He took the hand in his and fought the urge to envelop it in both to feel its warmth and significance. He nodded frantically in affirmations of everything and nothing… of the moment. He looked at Starr as if to ensure that there was a witness and ensure himself that it was real.

"I read all about how you shot and killed your first man when you was twelve," Rufus said. "They say you killed more the law don't even know about by the time you was fifteen."

"White men, too," Starr added.

"How do you like our white Indian," Bill said, pointing to Starr.

"A man is more than what's on the outside. You remember that, boy."

"Hates white men with a passion. Too bad he is one. One day he'll have to blow his own head off."

"The judiciary is doing all in its power to make that unnecessary."

Bill sat down on his cot while Starr leaned himself comfortably against the cell bars. Rufus stood alone in the middle of the cell. Bill spat chew against the wall.

"What you want with me?" Bill asked.

Taken aback, Rufus looked to Starr for assistance but got a sly grin. After a moment of panic, he conjured the grit to answer.

"I wanna know what it's like."

"To be me?" Bill smiled.

"A real Indian, not doin' with white folks."

Bill looked at Starr, a bit impressed. He thought about it for a moment. "I ain't thought of it like that," Bill said. "I guess it's true that I don't ride much with the herd."

"I told you," Starr interjected. "I told you."

"I just done what I done," Bill said. "Never thought much about it."

"Didn't you know early on that you was gonna be a great outlaw?" Rufus asked.

"When I was twelve years old, I shot my brother-in-law 'cause he was a jackass liked to knock folks around. Just happened. My parents left when I was seven. Happened. That's all. I did what I did an' what I wanted."

Rufus smiled and rushed toward Bill's cot. "That's what I'm talkin' about. Doin' what you want. You and the Cook brothers and Ned Christie and Apache Kid..."

"What he means, Bill," Starr said, "is Indians livin' as free men, right? In our own Territory, right?

Rufus nodded vigorously.

"Men in their own Territory in the open land," Starr clarified.

"No one like Callahan whuppin' you for speakin' Creek or readin' about folks like you."

"Who's Callahan?" asked Bill.

"He ran the Mission School I went to. I took his whip from him and hit him with it. He said I was damned."

"Join the crowd, boy," Bill said with a wave of the hand indicating all of Murderer's Row. "They didn't think much of my salvation at my Indian school neither."

"All damned by white men," added Starr.

"It ain't right," said Rufus.

Bill was surprised at a soft note of anger inside him. A bit of outrage. He'd been listening to Starr too long, he thought. But nonetheless, there it was. White men had chased him for most of his life. His Daddy ran to Indian Territory after the war to escape a lynching for siding with the Union. When they wanted to hang him for protecting his colored soldiers from white hunters and cowboys, he went AWOL. Alone with his mother, Bill bounced from here to there, mostly raised by an old Negro woman when he wasn't imprisoned in some Indian School full of God and white men. He looked at Buck and wondered if he had lived a similar life. He felt a sympathy for the boy and a little sorry for himself. He literally shook his head to free himself from both.

"No, it ain't right," Starr reiterated.

"You shut up white man." Sympathy for the boy and sorry for himself. Both annoyed him. Of late, he had suffered these sentimental intrusions. Scheduled to die in a month's time, he felt weakened. He doubted himself. He had never feared anything because he knew without thinking that one thing happened and then another and another and there wasn't a damned thing a man could do about any of it. Now, he lost the only shelter and comfort he had ever known: the firm knowledge that it was all a series of unrelated, unmotivated and random happenings. He now put one event before another and they seemed to tell a story, leading here. It had started with, "if I had done this, then maybe that," which made it seem as if he had control and it was all his own doing as opposed to events that heaven and earth conjured with the whimsicality of Spring weather. Inside the shelter of seeing it all beyond his power, he had floated above fear; and fearlessness let him do what he wanted and take what he had to. In a world of infinite indifference and utter randomness, nothing mattered. Not his Daddy, not his Ma. Killing didn't matter. It happened, like lightning. Men died. A bullet was no different from falling off a cliff. Men were no more or less dead either way. But now he felt fear, and he couldn't tell if it welled up from wanting to live or horror at dying. Starr should not have convinced him to talk to this boy. It was May 17th and he would hang on June 25th. At this point, escape plans only embellished his desperation.

"I got my own gang now, outside o' Tulseytown or Okmulgee," Rufus spoke into the long pause. "If you all escape you can join up with us. We only done liquor so far, but there's five of us an' we can do a lot more."

"I don't want to die here," Bill said as he lay back on his cot and turned his face toward the wall. Fear had changed him. Acknowledging it was hateful to him. It diminished him in his own eyes.

"Amen," Starr added to Bill's first full-throated affirmation of his plan. Starr placed his arm around Rufus' shoulder and accompanied him from the cell. "Let Bill rest," he said. "Bill's been doin' a lot o' thinkin'. You and me," he added as he patted Buck's shoulder, "you an' me got things to talk about."

4

How have all those exquisite adaptations of one part of the organisation to another part, and to the conditions of life and of one organic being to another being, been perfected? We see these beautiful co-adaptations most plainly in the woodpecker and the mistletoe; and only a little less plainly in the humblest parasite which clings to the hairs of a quadruped or feathers of a bird; in the structure of the beetle which dives through the water; in the plumed seed which is wafted by the gentlest breeze; in short, we see beautiful adaptations everywhere and in every part of the organic world.

- Charles Darwin
"The Origin of Species"

"The first one at the ranch, the colored man… he was acrawlin' and amoanin' after he got gutshot the first time. I saw the blood pourin' out o' him. I never seen so much. I seen little bits come outta me an' it stopped so I'd pick the little hard bit off to see some more but that man poured it all over the ground. I wondered if you could plant something in it an' it would grow and would it be red but I didn't have nothin' to plant. I went up to him an' looked at his face to see what it looked like an' I laughed. He was all dark 'cause o' bein' a nigger and wet from sweat and he had white patches from the dust that stuck. He was a spotty face. I seen a clown before so I laughed. The others didn't. I guess they never seen clowns. I kicked him with my foot to see if he turned over like I done with half dead critters I seen but he didn't so I told 'em that he wouldn't an' they said to just kick him harder and push him over so I did. He was like big bug on his back, his legs all twitchin'. The shirt on his chest was all soakin' red and he was gushin' more. I bent down to look close. I tol' the rest of 'em to come see, but they didn't. He gushed blood like someone was pumpin' the handle… whooshhh… whoooshhh. I think they was chicken. I touched it and it felt warm and good. I put my whole hand there. He moaned when I felt the little hole and the tear in the cloth. Then I felt the hole in his belly 'cause I wanted

to see how deep it was. I put my finger in it and it went all the way in. I pulled my hand up an' it was red. I showed it to 'em an' they all kinda moved away so I chased 'em. I was gonna brand 'em with my red hand. They ran and I chased 'em."

- Theodosia Swain

Having alluded to the subject of reversion, I may here refer to a statement often made by naturalists--namely, that our domestic varieties, when run wild, gradually but invariably revert in character to their aboriginal stocks.

- Charles Darwin
"The Origin of Species"

Armed with his new and extraordinary mission to free Cherokee Bill and thus give birth to the greatest gang of Indian outlaws that the Territory—or the world—had ever known, Rufus swelled in his own estimation. He drew closer to his heretofore nebulous vision of himself as redeemer of men like Bill, Henry Starr, his father. Redeemer of the hopelessly ravaged and the unjustly damned.

This was a man's grave task, but he attacked it with a boy's buoyant spirits. He determinedly marched about the prison. He worked to hide the fact that he was laden with great secrets. He kept an even temper; but he wore his status proudly nonetheless. Prisoners read his newfound gravitas as recognition of the strange reputation he'd gained for sycophancy gilded with a uniquely carefree brutality.

"What you all puffed up about?" his cell mate slurred at him.

Rufus ignored him.

"You get to your precious Nigger Bill?"

Rufus pulled the makeshift truncheon from his pants and brandished it.

"You keep it up," he threatened.

The cell mate swigged from his bottle, trying to swallow his fear of a boy he once mocked.

Rufus was all eyes now. He watched the guards' and turnkeys' comings and goings. He noted the inmates' routines on every floor and the Trustees' methods of disposing their duties. They had six weeks. Just six weeks. It was the middle of May and Bill would be dead in late June.

Starr was charged with procuring a gun, the most important and difficult task. He knew that none of the guards or turnkeys would get him one—no matter how much he paid—for fear he'd shoot them with it. Most of the prisoners were drunk or crazy and trustworthy as snakes. He wrote coded letters to contacts on the outside—queries on the imminent death of a sickly relation and the urgent need for hard-to-procure medicines, but he got no response until he learned that a cohort of one of his former cohorts, serving time on the second floor, would be released on June 3rd. Rufus served as go-between. Through Rufus, Starr negotiated a price with the soon-to-be-released prisoner to secure a revolver and some shells. Based on his observations of prison routine, Rufus told the inmate to drop the equipment in the outhouse lime stored near the cesspit. When the buckets were dumped, Trustee's threw a shovelful of lime on top. A harsh substance, no one touched it, and more importantly, no one sifted it for contraband as they did with piles of dirt, bulk foodstuffs and the like.

They waited. First they waited a week for the prisoner to gain his freedom. When his release date came and went, they waited for word of the gun. None came. After several days, Starr grew nervous. He started scrambling for another way to procure a gun. Escape plans were like lice in that prison—

crawling on every head—and he talked up the remaining candidates, the one's he hadn't touched before, men lower on the hierarchy; he felt nervous at his reduction to querying lesser men with shorter chances of success. He never told anyone that Cherokee Bill was part of the plan. The information would have been a surer road to the informant's early release than any escape attempt.

A few days later, Starr found his plan B. A half-drunk Trustee named Sherman Vann insisted he could smuggle a gun inside the prison. As Starr assumed he would, Vann insisted that he and his buddy come along. Out of options, Starr agreed. He told Bill, fearing a tirade. Bill hated sudden changes of plan and trusted very few, but Bill glared at Starr, and said nothing. In 13 days he was scheduled to hang.

On Sunday, June 16th Starr approached Sherman Vann to get the gun. Vann showed up with a rotten-toothed, shit-eating grin instead.

"I'll keep ahold of it," he smirked.

Starr breathed deeply to maintain his composure. "That was not the agreement," he seethed as he considered what to do. "But I am a flexible man," he said steadily after a pause and a moment's reflection. "And it's my plan, which you don't have. Without it, you'll just get shot before the hangman gets you. So I got nothin' to fear from you. You can keep the gun until… ," Starr considered a moment, "… Friday. Then you'll give it to me, and I'll share the plan with you."

"You want me to get it from him?" Rufus demanded on learning of the treachery.

"No. You do somethin' and he'll just run to the Deputies. Let it lie," Starr said, secure that he had appealed to Vann's self-interest. "Just let it lie."

Nonetheless, Rufus spied on Vann. He went where Vann went and searched wherever he left; but he never found the gun. He repeated the appeal to beat the hell out of him, but Starr insisted that Bill wouldn't want it.

The guards locked the prisoners in their cells each night. Bill's cell was at the end of the first floor corridor. He was one of the last locked up. He planned to stuff some wadding into the keyhole, making it impossible to lock the cell. When both night turnkeys gathered to fix it, he'd grab the gun and jump them. He'd free Starr and they would run.

They chose a Sunday. Even the murderers were low-key on Sunday—the turnkeys less alert. "Somethin' about the Lord does it," Starr had smiled, "keeps 'em slow an' simple."

On the appointed Friday, Starr approached Sherman Vann.

"What you want?" Vann asked irritably.

Starr did not reply. He knew he didn't need to.

"I don't know whatchu want," Vann continued. "I surely don't know."

"You need to gimme that gun."

Vann shook his head like an ill-tempered child. "I can't," he finally choked out. "It got stole."

Starr's pulse rose. He felt the blood tingle beneath the skin on his face.

"I ain't lyin I swear. I been lookin' for it up an' down and I can't find it. I don't know who took it. I didn't tell no one."

Starr grabbed Vann's neck, rammed his shoulder into him, slamming him hard against the wall. "Are you lyin' to me?" He grabbed Vann's hair and smacked his head against the brick. It left a bloody smear.

"I ain't lyin," Van blurted.

"When?"

"Two days ago."

Starr smacked Vann's head against the wall again.

"You didn't say nothin'?"

"I was tryin' to get it back. I thought I could."

Starr gave the bloodied head one more smack against the wall. Vann crumpled to the ground. "You are too stupid to kill," he said. Starr looked up the corridor. His violence had not attracted much attention and there wasn't a guard in sight. As he returned to his cell, he knew that he had two days to find another gun. He also knew that he couldn't. It had taken him weeks to get hold of one he'd found and that happened so quickly and sloppily, it blew up in his face. He could try later, his internal euphemism for 'after Bill had hanged,' but he wouldn't have the much-feared and very deadly Cherokee Bill at his side. With Bill, Starr's chances of escape increased dramatically. Without him, the turnkeys would be far less cowed and far more aggressive in pursuit. His own odds of escape had diminished, Starr thought with a twinge of unselfish sadness, but due to the lateness of the hour, Bill's had disappeared.

Starr told Rufus first. The boy said nothing before he turned on his heel and walked away. After a moment, Starr chose to follow him, fearing the worst. Rufus tromped straight to Vann's cell and found the bloodied drunk inside. From his pocket, Rufus pulled his truncheon and swung it against the side of Vann's face. Blood sprayed across the cot. Rufus raised the weapon again but Starr grabbed him and dragged him from the cell.

"We gotta tell Bill," Starr said, shaking Rufus from his rage.

Rufus broke free. He stood stock still in the hallway of Murderer's Row. A helpless look came over him. Then he wept. A shocked Starr looked on. Immediately he realized that the boy wasn't crying for himself. Never in his life had he seen one man's tears for another. He had seen men shot over pennies, but he had never seen this. He almost smiled.

"You be cryin' if it was me?" he asked, knowing the answer and not expecting one. He tentatively brushed the boy's shoulder in the way of a comforting gesture, but that was all he could do. Sobbing sounds transformed into animal grunts as Rufus gritted his teeth and brought himself to heel. He stood erect again and swiped his eyes and nose with his sleeve.

"We gotta tell Bill," Buck repeated.

They walked funereally through the corridor's aimlessness and drunkenness. They found Bill waiting on his cot.

"What happened?" He asked as if he already knew that it had all gone wrong.

"The gun got stole," Starr said.

Another tear rolled down Rufus' cheek. Seeing it, Bill smiled and shook his head. This was the damnedest boy. 'Too bad he won't be at my funeral,' Bill thought, 'someone cryin' for me would make pretty a picture.'

"My fault," Starr said. "I shoulda took it right away. Shouldn't o' left it with him."

"Everybody dies," said Bill. "I had my run." He laid back on his cot and put his arms behind his head. His open eyes stared up at the ceiling as if it were a star-filled sky.

The rest of Sunday came and went. Rufus saw neither Bill nor Starr. He went about his Trustee chores and worked to think of nothing but the broom's dust or the bucket's filth. He felt like he'd been hollowed out and left behind.

On Monday he looked into the courtyard and saw men preparing the gallows. He thought of going to see Bill, but something in him didn't want to. He was scared, afraid of what might happen. He had cried. He might do it again. Bill might be scared. Bill's life had been immortalized in books and his death would be equal to his life if Rufus had anything to do with it. If he had known without the slightest doubt that Bill would play his part and await the Final Judgment with the implacability of a martyred saint, he would not have hesitated to visit him. But he had doubts. He doubted himself, and deep down something inside him even doubted Bill. After all, he wasn't just a legend any more. Rufus had touched his flesh, watched him piss and seen him turn his head away in trepidation. He had become something less than the legend. He was a man. And so to prepare for Bill's death, Rufus had to make him a myth again. He wanted to forget that he had touched Bill's flesh. Again it would be like a tale in a storybook. It wouldn't hurt so bad that way. It was proper, he decided, that his next sight of Bill would be on the gallows.

With the prisoners still locked in their cells on the morning of Tuesday, June 25th, head jailer J.D. Berry with two guards on either side walked to Bill's cell. They stood before it, and with barely a glance at the man inside, Berry read from a letter.

"The review of the conviction of Crawford Goldsby for the murder of Ernest Melton remains in the hands of the Supreme Court of the United States. Judge Isaac Charles

Parker therefore grants a stay of execution pending completion of that review."

The jailer and his Deputies then marched just as quickly from the jailhouse corridor. Berry's voice had woken Bill. He had been half asleep when the jailer started talking, but he had understood. He would not die today.

"Bill done got Supereemed ," hollered one prisoner. Whoops and hollers echoed on Murderer's Row.

"Hooray for the Supereem Court," another shouted as laughter exploded up and down the prison.

On that day, there was no milling about in the halls of the Ft. Smith jail. The guards left the prisoners in their cells. They always did on hanging day.

~

On hearing that he would not die, Bill breathed. He felt the air inflate his lungs, his chest swell full of it.

"Now how we gonna get the hell outta here," he winked at Starr on seeing him. Henry had to stop himself from hugging Bill. He thanked God he'd hitched his star to this relentless force and damned lucky sonofabitch.

A legend about whom he had only read, a flesh and blood man whose hand he had taken, a legend again on the certainty of his death. And now, once more, Bill lived. He had died by all rights. Rufus had seen Bill to the gallows; he'd envisioned his corpse hung from a rope and now Bill stood before him more alive than ever. Rufus examined the resurrected man from his smiling face to his bootless feet. He had never been more awed before anyone.

The day after Bill's reprieve, Rufus learned that he himself would be released on July 4th. Starr noted the irony.

"You get free on the same say as they celebrate America free. Look what they done with it. I'm jus' remindin' you to show equal mercy."

With Bill's reprieve, there was time to execute Starr's new escape plan. Rufus didn't have many days left, and he wanted to be a part of it. Bill, though, had prepared himself to die and had to cope with living to face dying again. He had reasoned and struggled with imminent death, and, finally, he had learned to sleep soundly with it. Now, as if he hadn't already faced down fear and forced himself to live through dying with a downright celestial calm, the reprieve and prospect of conquering that dread yet again, it choked him. Having come close to the fire, having felt its heat, he couldn't will it away twice. You have to know something to truly dread it. Now he knew proximity to death. Fear had crept up on him the last time, stealthily, and had remained pleasantly vague; and then he replaced it with rage at thwarted plans and cursing the world for showing him a fool who couldn't even hold onto a gun. He hadn't had time to fear a slow march to a hanging until he was so mad at himself and the world that it didn't seem to matter anymore. But now the reprieve had come. His rage was spent. A new, more rational plan had been set in motion and he waited again, to die or not—again. And this time, he brooded on his own fear. He had seen the men marched before the crowds in the jail's courtyard, the noose dangling all alone beneath the strangely grand leanto, like a fancy bauble in a high-toned shop. The crowds chatted and milled with anticipation. Ft. Smith had good hangmen. Men usually died quickly from broken necks instead of writhing and jerking for endless minutes at the end of the rope. Bill wondered if they'd cheer when his hangman pulled the lever.

To exorcise his fear, to familiarize himself with its object and thus reduce it to the level of a bullet or a gun or a horse or all the other things that could kill him and about which he didn't give a shit, Bill closed his eyes and held his breath. He laid still and filtered out the noise and stink of the men all around him. He tried to anticipate the nothing there could be when he died. That's what scared him—nothing. He knew pain; he had felt it. But no matter how hard he tried he could not imagine nothing. He could not grasp not being here. He had always been here. There was no opposite. It was unthinkable. It was beyond belief. But still he closed his eyes and held his breath and filtered out the sounds and smells to bring himself closer to it, like a blind man groping at a face. He would know nothingness before nothingness would mean he could not. He had seen men play a game called chess. He had seen them concentrate for hours the way he would for moments as he aimed his gun. They said it was a puzzle. He decided that this too, was a puzzle. He had only to concentrate hard enough and he would solve it. He would come to understand what nothing was. At night he chiseled silently at the brickwork supporting the cell's metal doors. He hacked at the mortar to remove bricks and enlarge the empty space behind where he would hide the long-awaited gun. All night he concentrated on soundlessly sweeping up and moistening the mortar dust to spread along the bricks so that no one would notice. During the day he puzzled and rarely slept.

From Bill, Starr tried to hide his own uncertainty, disguise his chafing at the wait and his guilt about his former failure. He redoubled his outward insouciance, behaving with the confident panache of a cheating gambler in a game full of rubes. Regardless, Bill grew less responsive and spent more of his daylight hours with arms folded tightly across his chest. He rarely left his cell. He paced doggedly or lay on his cot as still as a dead man.

On July 2, five days before Rufus was to leave the jail, a guard approached Starr.

"You got a visitor," he said.

"She's here," Starr whispered as he flew past Bill's cell behind the guard. Bill's eyes popped open and he sat upright. Rufus, watching, almost chased Starr down the corridor until he caught himself. Starr deliberately slowed his pace and pulled a cigarette from his breast pocket. He stopped for a moment to light it, with the impatient guard looking on.

"Move it along, Henry," said the guard as Starr finally passed him. The woman in question sat in Henry's cell with a handkerchief to her nose and unquiet eyes. Clean clothes and Sunday best marked her as a proper lady and she was shown due deference. She tried to avert her eyes from the dirty men who gathered outside the cell openly gawking at her. Some displayed stiff manhoods expanding their trousers while others leeringly stroked their conspicuous bulges. The guard roughly pushed them aside as he led Henry in. She stood as he entered. He paused on seeing her. The stranger took one awkward step forward, urging him with her eyes. He then stepped toward her and hesitantly placed his hands on her arms with reluctant familiarity. She turned her cheek toward him and he leaned daintily forward to kiss it. The guard parked himself nearby as the lady resumed her seat. They made awkward small talk about non-existent people for a few minutes. Finally, the lady professed to be overtaken by the jailhouse redolence and minced quickly from the cell. Rufus watched her go, and knew that the guns were waiting. He had half a day before he was scheduled to empty more shitters. That's when he'd collect the gun and shells. In the meantime, he returned to Bill's cell. Starr joined them. In silence the brethren admired each other, a satisfied nod and a flick of a grin the only clue to their conspiracy.

For the remaining days before Rufus left, they never mentioned the plan. They spent their time in pregnant silence. On Rufus' departure date, they shook hands in Bill's cell and subtly acknowledged that they would see each other soon. Henry felt almost sorry for the boy as he left Ft. Smith jail, anticipating his reunion with the great Cherokee Bill. Starr knew that, despite the promises and assurances, neither he nor Bill would probably ever see Rufus Buck again. Starr planned to escape the Territory on the fastest wings he could find. He neither knew, nor cared what Bill would do, but felt confident it did not include Rufus Buck and his gang.

If he had been asked to think about it though, he would have decided that he wished Buck well.

~ ~ ~

John Buck waited outside in the familiar old wagon with familiar old mare as Rufus stepped from the Ft. Smith jail. Surprised, Rufus stopped on seeing him, acknowledging how far he had traveled from his days as a child of parents. The mare and the wagon and the man inside were like spectral visitations, not unwelcome, but eerie and reeking of things past. As Rufus approached his father, the latter nodded to him with a hint of a smile.

"Your Ma showed me your letter, so I came," he said.

"Thanks," Rufus replied as he climbed on board.

His father snapped the reins and the horse moved on. Both men stared at the road ahead. Neither spoke.

Rufus scanned the land all around. He wanted to see if he sensed any difference as he crossed the river boundary from Arkansas into the Indian Territory. Would the air be sweeter? The soil a deeper, richer brown? Cooler air touched him as they approached the water, and its whispers made for the sweetest listening he'd had for ninety days. As they crossed the cool river, the demarcation, they entered a thicket of brush and oak. Shade and the buzz of insects and the bird's chirping and squawking added to the soft cacophony that tickled Rufus' ears. As the road progressed, the land opened up before him. And he was home. Starr had told him about it. He saw it with new eyes and it was among the most perfect and beautiful things he had ever seen.

"I learned some stuff in prison, Pa."

He looked at his father and got no response.

"I learned about the Territory an' how it's supposed to be."

His father gazed at the road ahead. Rufus followed the gaze as he spoke, eyeing the beauty and birthright that he would reclaim.

"I met Cherokee Bill." At this, his father cast him a glance. "He's a good man. Nobody tells him how to live or where. He lives like white folks." Rufus looked at his father's impassive profile. "I wanna be like him."

His father's face relaxed into an acquiescence laced with sadness. Rufus hoped that the look was not indicative of yet another blow from the brutal inevitabilities under which his father had suffered all of his life. Rufus tried to see contentment in that old face, a flicker of acceptance—and maybe even hope—for which he could take credit as the dutiful son; and he may have seen it. But he could not be sure.

~

Bill's ill temper did not go unnoticed. A powerful presence, his mood bled beyond his cell. It infected the inmates like fear infects a herd. The guards grew tense. Simultaneously, one of the men who had smuggled guns to Starr found it impossible to contain his brush with fame. In terms general enough to salve his conscience and reduce fear of retaliation from Starr or his associates, he desperately boasted his part in the play.

"I can jus' tell you," he said to any available Ft. Smith listener, "you keep your eye on the Ft. Smith jail. There some mighty wicked fellas might come flyin' outta there." He'd laugh and clap his hands. "And I bet you ain't never gonna look at a cesspit quite the same," which left his audience half-amused because they sensed a dirty joke and half-befuddled because they couldn't find it.

The rumors of imminent jailbreak spread quickly throughout Ft. Smith. They reached the local press, and finally the head jailer's ears. Coupled with Bill's agitation and its contagious effect on the jail population, the jailer sensed trouble and feared the worse. Determined that there would be no break on his watch, on July 10th he ordered all prisoners locked in their cells and the entire prison searched.

The dramatic lockdown and search agitated the inmates on every floor. The deputies stormed from cell to cell amidst the prisoners' queries, resentments and taunts. They searched clothes, boots, felt every inch of mattresses and even stirred shit buckets for telltale clanks and obstructions. They found knives, manufactured and homemade. They found whiskey aplenty, most of it originally jailer-supplied, and now jailer-confiscated to enormous complaint and occasional violent resistance.

Bill waited his turn. He checked the brick wall and it looked undisturbed enough to fool any guard. He pawed over the thin mattress and he could feel the little lumps, but he knew what he was looking for. He hoped that ignorance would make them undetectable. He laid on his cot, surprised at his own demeanor. For the first time in some time he felt calm.

Two guards unlocked his cell and ordered him out. One stood by him in the corridor while the other conducted the search. Bill looked up and down the empty hallway. He rarely saw it empty. This is how it would look when he made his escape. From within the cell he heard the rufflings and tearings. A moment later, the guard emerged with a triumphant smile holding a handful of six-gun cartridges.

"Bill was plannin' a party," the guard mocked. Bill spat tobacco on the wall.

The other guard shoved Bill back in his cell where his few belongings sat in disarray and his mattress stuffing protruded from a huge gash down its middle. He turned to face the bars as the guards closed them. The brick wall was untouched, its contents undisturbed.

5

Rufus' old house surprised him as he approached it. It looked smaller than he remembered. He would have sworn the wood had been less weathered, its dimensions more imposing. The big shade tree looked bare of leaves despite high summer and the chickens pecking the ground less plump and more desperate for what morsels the earth offered up. His father pulled the horse to a stop and his mother filled the open doorway. She waved courteously at him and he waved back. There was no smile on her face. Rufus realized that he wasn't wearing one either. Looking at her, this did not feel like a homecoming. It felt like goodbye.

He jumped from the wagon and walked toward the dour woman. He walked as if he would go right through her. If he could, he would have—to feel every inch and muscle of her, to know her finally. She put her arms around him and held him tight. Her fist pounded hard on his back as she held him. Then, having mastered whatever that fist smashed down, she let him go.

"Them boys were here," she said. "They's gonna meet you in Okmulgee." She started back into the house, but turned again. "They was wearin' guns," she added.

Rufus' father led the horse and carriage toward the barn. Rufus watched him go, and surveyed the house, the fields, and the distant trees. He made a picture of it to hold onto as if it were a special place he had run across and wouldn't see again. He felt lonely because he knew he didn't belong here anymore, and had no other home. It was hard to imagine his parents without him. He couldn't see their lives continue—their sun and moon continue to rise—without him as their fulcrum. What would they do with their days? Without him, they might be mere shadows. Neither seemed whole, not like Cherokee Bill or Henry Starr who grabbed what they wanted and captured the world's imagination doing it. They were all about possibility. His mother and father, on the other hand, took nothing, and had nothing—except him. And now he would leave them and they would continue, less substantial, ineffectually scratching and clawing at the earth like the scrawny chickens pecking at the place. He went into the house and put a few things into an old saddlebag. He took a final look at his father's heirlooms of loss hanging on the wall. He wondered if he belonged up there with the piece of bagpipe; or maybe his parents did—heirlooms. Maybe, he thought, his father had been mourning himself all this time. His mother passed through on her way to the stove. She paused to note the saddlebag on the floor but did not glance at her son as she continued on her way. This was her goodbye.

~

After the guards discovered Bill's bullets, Starr wanted to reschedule the escape attempt, but Bill refused. "Friday," Bill insisted. It was Friday this time due to the Vann's knowledge of the previous Sunday plan. Starr didn't argue. Bill was the linchpin, and he wanted Bill happy. When you got right down to it, Sunday or Friday didn't matter much. The Ft. Smith jail needed time to relax. After all the excitement of the rumors and the search, the guards needed to slip back to the their usual complacency. The flow of contraband needed to fully resume and the prisoners had to stop yammering about the gun that had been found inside a bucket of lime in the downstairs privy. On hearing of it, Bill and Henry knew that it was their gun—the gun that Sherman Vann had lost and that should have freed them by now.

"If that boy was still here," Starr laughed, "he would not rest until he found the sonofabitch who stole the gun, or some sonofabitch he thought mighta stole it and kicked the shit out of him."

Bill Smiled.

"I wonder what he's up to?" Starr added. Bill didn't answer.

"Don't you wonder?"

"Ain't got nothin' to do with me," Bill replied.

With his back to Bill, Starr smiled with satisfaction and shook his head knowingly. "I thought you was gonna ride with him."

"You too," parried Bill.

"Yeah, but I ain't his hero an' all."

"An' I didn't ask to be. So why don't you shut up about it."

"You feelin' a little guilty about that?"

"I don' owe nobody nothin' an' I said to shut up about it."

After a while, Starr broke the silence. "The week after next oughta do it," he said, signaling satisfaction with the appointed date. "That oughta give 'em all time to simmer down. And they won't expect nothin' so soon."

Bill nodded vaguely. He had gotten used to having Rufus around. He had grown accustomed to the flattery. He had never thought about riding with him one way or another—never took it seriously enough. When Henry told him how Rufus might help get a gun and the boy, in fact, proved useful, Bill thought about taking him on. Why not? The boy had done him a good turn. But now he was gone and the plan moved on without him. It would take commitment and a solid effort to track him down. It would take even more to teach him up so that he could do the job without getting things killed that Bill didn't want dead. He was gone now, so there was no cause to think about it. He was part of the past, just another player in the pageant of happenstance that Bill marched innocently through. Gone or dead didn't much matter. It was done. You didn't go running after it any more than you would a bullet that passed you by.

~

John Buck walked a bay gelding toward the front of the house. He stopped Rufus and gestured to the horse. "Go on. Take it," he said. He patted the horse and ran his hand briefly along its flank as if saying goodbye to the horse instead of his son. And then in one of his most rare gestures, he looked his son in the eye. His features sat motionless and overwhelming. Without a word or movement, he asked where his son was going, what had happened to him, told him to go and wished him well, and mourned the fate he feared awaited him—all in a single swish of the horse's tail against the omnipresent flies. Knowing there were no answers, John Buck entered his house. Rufus climbed on the horse and began his forty-mile trek to Okmulgee.

~

The hullabaloo surrounding the prison search dulled Bill's anxiety. He thought less about the enormity of nothing. Guards finding some of his shells but missing the gun behind his cell's loose bricks proved a rare, prescient sort of luck. So nothing stood in his way. He began to believe that he'd soon be out in the world and doing as he pleased. On Murderer's Row, his newfound self-possession proved as notable as his tension had been.

"What is Bill gonna do when he's outta here?" Starr teasingly asked him, daring to contemplate a future.

Bill had considered it. "I'm gonna visit Ike Rogers," he said. Rogers was the man who had informed on him and set him up for capture by the Marshals. He owed Ike Rogers. "Once I take care o' that, I don't know. Think I'll leave the Territory. West. Texas, maybe."

"I'm thinkin' California," Starr mused. "San Francisco sounds like a place for a man of my quality."

"They prize bullshit there?"

"I do think they might," Starr smiled proudly. "I do think they might."

As the day approached, Bill tread carefully. He foresaw another attack of that cowardly fearfulness to which he'd once succumbed. He watched his hands, holding one out before him and waiting for the tiniest tremor. Seeing none, he'd relax. Each day without the sick feeling in his stomach or a trembling hand gave him confidence that he could resume his life as the man he had been. That he had once faltered... he'd have to live with that, like a physical defect, a bum leg that he knew might go out on him. He would just have to live with it.

~

Arriving in Okmulgee on July 11, Rufus listened. He listened to the talk. Ever since he was a kid he had known you could find out what was happening by listening to folks passing by, overhearing the ones sitting outside the blacksmith or the dry goods store. To his surprise and alarm, today they talked of Bill. They talked of "catching" Bill. His mouth dry, he found a copy of the The Ft. Smith Elevator posted as ever in an Okmulgee main street window. He read the article. It described the jail lockdown, search and discovery of a revolver hidden in an indoor bucket of lime. It said they found bullets in Cherokee Bill's cell.

That was all it said. Shaking, barely breathing, Rufus searched all over the page for more, but there was nothing. Bill hadn't hidden his gun in any lime. The article didn't mention the wall, or the gun that Bill had hidden there. His breathing slowed. The trembling slipped off of him. He calmly considered what the newspaper hadn't said: It didn't say that they'd found Bill's gun. Had Bill moved his gun to another hiding place? A bucket of lime? That wasn't like Bill; he stuck with things. He had hidden his gun in the wall, and that's where it would have stayed.

Rufus turned from the window having convinced himself that Bill was safe, that the newspaper didn't write about the gun because the guards hadn't found it. The gun in the lime could have belonged to anyone.

Comforted, he walked through the town regarding its people. Even the dandies no longer seemed bright butterflies; and even if they were, he was the snake that ate them. If they knew what was coming, he thought, they'd cower, guns at the ready to fend off the righteous vengeance headed straight for them. He mounted his horse to look for his men. Only the slightest twinge of doubt disturbed him.

One of the first things Rufus had to do upon returning to his gang was beat the crap out of Maoma July.

"Whatchu tellin' us what to do for? You ain't even been here."

"This the Maoma July gang now?" Rufus mocked.

"Maybe it ought be..." Maoma mumbled.

Maoma had prepared meticulously for his leader's return. He and Sam Sampson hadn't seen much of Lewis and Luckey since Rufus' imprisonment. The pairs had gone their separate ways. Only upon checking with Mrs. Buck, which he did with metronomic regularity, and learning of Rufus' imminent release did Maoma and Sam seek the others out.

"We gotta get ready," Maoma excitedly exclaimed. "He's comin' back."

Maoma had taken the liberty of stealing guns. With Sam he shared a makeshift leanto in the woods outside Okmulgee. Inside was an old chest he had filled with a substantial cache of stolen revolvers, rifles and bullets in preparation for the gang's reunion. He proudly displayed the guns to Lewis and Luckey as he outlined the next step.

"We need some horses," he said. With great care, he planned a nighttime raid on a small farm owned by an elderly man up toward Baldhill who had once offended him. Despite the farm's sole occupants being an old man and his equally old wife, the four managed to steal only two equally old, swayback horses and had to dissuade the owner from pursuit with a hail of revolver fire.

When Rufus returned, he wore a newfound air of majesty and poise. It impressed Maoma. It fulfilled his expectations of what a leader should be as it simultaneously stoked his jealousy.

"We are gonna ride with Cherokee Bill," Rufus proudly told them. "I brought him the gun he's gonna use to bust out, and then we'll be with his gang, makin' a name for ourselves. Henry Starr, too, the train robber."

"We gonna rob trains?" an excited Luckey asked.

"We gonna rob whatever we want. Whatever Bill says."

"How come we gotta do what he says. It's our gang. He'd be in prison wasn't for you," Maoma snarled.

"Cause he's Cherokee Bill," replied Rufus.

Under his breath, Maoma mocked, "'Cause heee's Cherokee Bill."

At first, Rufus ignored him. He wanted to enlighten them as he had been enlightened. He wanted to open their eyes to injustices and the possibilities for righting them as his had been. He tried to tell them what Henry Starr had said.

"He tol' me all about what it's supposed to be like. Ain't supposed to be white folks here. The land supposed to be ours and we supposed to be able to do what we want here."

"It is ours. It's Indian Territory," Maoma insisted.

"White folks all over it," Rufus countered. "Own most of it."

"Still Indian Territory," Maoma needled.

"We supposed to be different," Rufus protested, growing more frustrated at his inability to convey what had been so powerfully impressed upon him. "We supposed to be free here."

"Ain't we free?" Lewis asked quietly. "Niggers ain't slaves no more."

"You full o' shit," Maoma spat. "Always been white people in Indian Territory."

"My father tol' me about when there wasn't an' so did Henry Starr."

"Then your father's as big a liar as he is."

Rufus lunged at him. Maoma did not believe what he had said. He had no idea who had been or had not been in Indian Territory. He said it to provoke a fight that he didn't expect to win. Like a horse, he tested; he wanted to know that his leader deserved the honor of leadership and was a better man than he. He smiled with triumph when Rufus attacked him. He fought madly, with the excess enthusiasm and lack of discipline that marked his every move; and through it, he unleashed his anger and confirmed his admiration for the better man. Exhausted, he soon found himself flat on the ground, Rufus' knee in his chest. He tasted his own blood as he suffered bruising blows to his stomach and sides.

"I gib uh," he panted through mangled lips. "I gib up."

Rufus slowly crept off of him. Maoma staggered to his feet.

"Ain't we free?" Lewis asked again intently, as if they had not been interrupted.

Rufus placed his hands on his hips to catch his breath as he fought for the words. "It ain't supposed to be like this," he said with more exhaustion than passion. "That's what Henry says. He says it oughta be like the folks my Daddy remembers. He had things... on his wall to remember 'em." Rufus grew emotional at the memory of his father's mute adoration of the treasured objects—some of the few times he had seemed present and unbroken. He looked at the four youths standing before him. Maoma reached to the ground to snatch a bug in his hand. Sam stared attentively yet blankly at him, and Lewis and Luckey exchanged glances with each other. Rufus waved his arm at the land surrounding their makeshift home and raised his voice.

"Like this," he said. "Nothin' here. Ain't no one supposed to be here but us. No white folks, no Mission School, nothin'. Just us. And what we want."

The four boys looked confusedly at each other, and then, tentatively, as if not knowing what to expect, at the landscape surrounding them, heretofore as invisible as air. As if they had just magically appeared, the boys noted particular trees and wild grasses, bushes rustling from critter activity beneath. The noises struck them, occasional leaves and crows yapping in the still, sun-baked sea of brown and untamed green.

"When you see a town full o' white folks an' they hangin' us to death and throwin' us in jail and doin' what they done... it ain't right." Rufus paused with his gang's eyes on him as he struggled not to cry at the mute pain that enveloped his house. His father's eyes, aghast and impenetrable, his mother's wordlessly brutal goodbye—they silenced him. They expected no better than the nothing they got and they had learned to live with it. Doing so had cost them their souls.

Maoma, Sam, Lewis and Luckey recognized the depth of emotion staring at them, but did not know what it meant. However, they offered deference and respect, as you would to a lion's low moan or a lone wolf's howl. They knew it was heartfelt, and they knew it bespoke a warning.

"When Bill gets out, we gonna change it," Rufus continued in a choked voice. He would change it, he thought, for his Ma and Pa. His father would find a voice and his mother her freedom. He would give them that.

He reviewed the four standing before him. Acknowledging the expressions of puzzlement and concern, he clarified. "We gonna take everything they got," he said, "and drive 'em outta here."

Maoma jumped in the air and loudly smacked his fist in his palm. Sam bounced up and down pounding on Maoma with congratulatory hands. Lewis and Luckey smiled at one another, finally appreciating the clarity and simplicity of the task ahead.

6

The gang had plenty of plans but only one good horse and two spent ones between the five of them.

"We got a whole Territory to ride," Rufus warned. He knew a well-stocked livery stable in Checotah. He had traveled there with his father. In Checotah, few knew him or his fellows as thieves and whiskey peddlers. They would not be among the first suspects tracked down.

Arriving on town's edge near dusk, they waited for nightfall and then for the livery, the dry goods store, the barbershop and all the other businesses to close for the night. When all they heard was the cry of the rail whistle and the faint rustle from the saloon, they moved. Leaving their horses tied up in some trees, they crept into town by the light of a full moon in a cloudless sky. Breaking into the livery was just a matter of quietly forcing a back door of the large barn. The six horses inside rustled at the noise. By the dim light through the open door, Lewis immediately worked to calm them, walking among them, whispering to them, lightly touching a velvet nose.

"Pick four good ones," Rufus said as he moved into the next room. He gestured at Maoma and Sam to follow.

"Get a light," Lewis whispered to Luckey. Lewis noted

the horses' conformations through the slatted stall gates. As the light arrived, he smiled, satisfied that his judgments in the darkness held true. He knew horses. He grabbed some lead rope hanging from the gate, slowly opened it and approached a small gelding. With its calm disposition and short stature it was perfect for Luckey. Lewis glanced at his friend, expecting him to shine at the prospect like a kid at a toy; but Luckey nervously watched the door, ignoring the horse, his arm holding the lantern straight up in the air.

In the next room, Rufus collected tack. From the corner of his eye he saw Maoma on Sam Sampson's back, miming whooping and whipping as Sam tossed his head and mock-galloped in small circles around a table full of bits and bridles.

Rufus wanted to yell and he wanted to laugh. "Get a saddle, both o' you," he hissed. Maoma dropped from Sam's back and ran to the most audacious saddle he saw, full of shiny silver tie and rigging accents. He grabbed it by the horn and cantle, heaved it to his chest and ran toward the back, leaving Sam scrambling to find a suitable saddle.

"Get that to Lewis and come back for more," Rufus stage-whispered to the retreating Maoma as he continued collected reins, cinches, bits and saddlebags and piling them on the floor. He knew they might never see such plenty again so he planned to take advantage. Sam left the room carting a saddle as Maoma returned. Rufus pointed to the pile on the floor. Maoma grabbed two armsful of tack and ran.

By the time Rufus finished piling and Maoma and Sam carting, Lewis was saddling the third horse. When Rufus returned to the stable with a saddlebag across his shoulder, he heard raised voices.

"I want this one on him," Maoma said too loudly, pointing at the silver-emblazoned saddle.

"This one's better. It's broke in for this horse and fits him right."

"I don't care 'bout the damned horse."

"You better or it'll buck you off and trample you dead."

"I'll shoot it," Maoma said, pulling the gun from his holster.

"Leave the goddam saddle," Rufus almost shouted. "Saddle the last of 'em and let's go," he said to Lewis.

Fuming, Maoma plastered an "I'll show them" look on his face, pulled his knife, and began to saw the silver buckles and spangles from the impressively ornate saddle.

"We're ready," Lewis announced. Four horses stood saddled.

"We'll walk 'em out," Rufus instructed. "Quiet."

"Gimme that light," Maoma commanded. Luckey handed it over and took his horses' reins from Lewis.

"Come on," said Rufus. He led the column out the door and into the moonlight and shadows.

Maoma still hacked at the thick leather to free the silver trinkets. "Ain't you comin'?" asked Sam, holding two increasingly restless horses watching their herd disappear.

"Hold this." Maoma gave the light to Sam. Both hands free, Maoma redoubled his efforts, breathlessly hacking at the saddle as if it were a carcass. Finally finished, he tucked the silver bits into the remaining horse's saddlebag and took the reins from Sam with a triumphant smile. Emboldened, he swung the lantern in a wide arc. Sam chuckled and Maoma let it go. The fire arced high and landed in a hay-filled corner. Sam danced a little hotfoot dance as the fire started and he ran his horse from the livery. An excited Sam paused to gawk at the flames until horses' wild whinnying jolted him. Two terrified horses reared in their stalls.

"What about them other horses?" Sam called to Maoma as he fled.

From 100 feet away, the rest of the gang looked back to see Maoma and Sam emerge with the glowing light behind them.

"What about them other horses?" Sam called again in an urgent whisper.

Seeing the flames, Lewis dropped his reins and ran back to the livery. Maoma jauntily trotted his horse up to the others.

"Where's he goin'?" he asked of Lewis. Soon two horses bolted from the barn, Lewis chasing hard after as the flames broke through to the outside of the building.

"C'mon," Rufus prodded as he jumped up on his horse. The others followed, galloping to the edge of town. The fire grew shockingly fast. As Lewis' horse, the last of them, gained its stride, he looked back and saw the whole livery building spewing flame. Alarmed voices echoed off the town's buildings. Bodies appeared, arms waving madly, black shadows against the burning light.

At a safe distance, Rufus slowed to a trot. As he did, Lewis rode past Maoma and shoved him, almost tipping him off his horse.

"Whadja do that for?" Maoma demanded.

"For almos' killin' them horses," Lewis hollered.

Maoma waved him off, "I knew you'd go get 'em," he mumbled in his own defense.

Rufus ignored them as he stared at the besieged town. Secure that they couldn't be seen, he watched the flames jump from the livery to the buildings on either side. The town bled orange firelight into the sky and smoke curled like giant puffs from the devil's own pipe. Even this far away, Rufus heard the faint remains of town folks' screams as the shadows ran back and forth, forming the long, ragged line of a bucket brigade. This was hell, Rufus thought as he watched them, as he watched them burn. This was it. The beginning. Watching the town burn and the townspeoples' frenzy to save it, he felt sad. Staring at the desperate men he realized the destruction he and his men would wreak. He didn't know why that saddened him. He had known that men would die. But that mattered less than the things he'd grown used to... the railroad station and the general store. Tulsey Town. It might all have to burn. Things he'd known all his life. He didn't know what kind of life he'd lead without them. He accepted on faith in Bill and Henry Starr that it would be a better one.

He turned away to see the wild and peaceful country glistening with moonlight. He forgot the hellish creatures dancing with the fire they had earned. He kept his eyes on the soft light. He rode on, trying to ignore the faint screaming behind him.

News of the theft and fire was soon the talk of the Territory. Half of Checotah's main street had burned. There was a great deal of speculation as to which of the Territory's long list of badmen bore responsibility. The name "Rufus Buck" did not occur.

~

"Whatchu doin?" Maoma asked.

Rufus sat cross-legged, hunched over paper full of crossed

out lines and scratchy minglings of small and capital letters. They were all bored. When Maoma and the others heard about the search of the Ft. Smith jail and the confiscation of Bill's bullets, Rufus convinced them that a few bullets were purposely left for the guards to find to distract them from the real booty. They had heard nothing from or about Bill since. Rufus traveled to Okmulgee every couple of days. The only literate one of the gang, he searched the Ft. Smith Elevator for news. On seeing nothing about Bill's escape, he hid his fear.

"Nothin' there," he'd beam. "That means on schedule."

"When's it gonna happen?" Lewis asked.

"Soon," Rufus replied. "Bill has to wait 'til it cools down from the search. Guards get all antsy for a while, watchin' every little thing. He gotta wait 'til it all goes regular again an' they ain't payin' much attention."

His men were bored but Rufus felt about to burst. He had to do something. He had willed an angel's visitation. He had made himself the savior of the great Cherokee Bill. Now he had to nudge fate again. So he huddled over his few sheets of paper, ink stained fingers scribbling his manifesto to the white men of Indian Territory.

"I'm workin'," he barked as Lewis interrupted with yet another question about Cherokee Bill. An hour later, Rufus summoned them all.

"I got somethin' for you all to hear," he called. As Maoma, Sam, Lewis and Luckey lumbered from sleep and ambled toward him, he held the paper and read in a clear, loud voice.

THis is A WArNing to ALL THe WHiTe Men in indiAn TerrtorY. IT is A TruMpet, cALing to ALL Indians to rise and drive THeM from our Land, Like the CAnoniTes in THe Bibl. We do noT, wAnT to HurT, nobodY, BuT We WiLL FigHT, and WHen oTHers, see WHaT We, HaVe done, THey WiLL, rise up, And ALL, WiLL, join us. THis, is fair WArning. If you LeaVe, you, WiLL noT, geT, HurT. If You sTaY, You, WiLL be cuT doWn. MY nAMe, is, Rufus Buck, And, Me and MY gang, do noT, fear AnY, MAn. We ainT scared of diYin. We, ainT, scared To, kiLL. For WHAT, You done To, mY faTHer, And, His before, You, don'T deserve, To be, Here.

Signed,
THe Rufus Buck gAng

He looked from his paper to his audience.

"We done?" Sam asked.

"I don't think they gonna leave," Lewis said.

"Me neither," Rufus replied.

"We gonna kill 'em all?"

"If we have to... when all the Indian and colored join us. White folks'd do the same if we took theirs."

Lewis nodded in understanding. Sam wearily trudged back to the leanto for the nap from which he'd been roused.

"The ones who leave," Maoma smiled, "We can jus' take what we want from what they leave behind, huh?"

"Sure," Rufus replied to Maoma's delight.

Alone at dusk, Rufus took his manifesto to Okmulgee. He rode through town as if strolling through a stage set deciding where to place a critical prop. He ignored the people. They didn't matter now. They would only matter tomorrow, as they crowded around to read it, as they frantically murmured to each other, aghast.

"Buck."

At his name, Rufus looked down to see Marshal John Garrett walking toward him. Garrett wore the smug, superior air common to Marshals approaching those over whom they had power. Rufus kept riding, barely having glanced at him.

"Hold on there," Garrett called, "We got business."

Rufus ignored him. Intent on the cataclysm that would soon engulf the Territory, Garrett was a persistent, buzzing fly, nothing more. It continued in Rufus' ear.

Garrett's quiet rage at being so publicly ignored grew, as did his consternation. Where, he wondered, did this boy gain the self-possession to disregard him? Any man would pay for that. For Buck, who had defied him once, there would be a particularly high price.

Oblivious to the threat, Rufus continued watchfully through town. He decided on Big Nellie's place, a rather grand two-story structure that sold everything from clothes to foodstuffs to livery goods. More people walked in and out of there than any other. More women and children. The fear would be greatest, the panic more palpable with women and children. Men would comfort them, trying to coo away the terror. He did not stop, but rode all the way through the town and out the other side. Safely out of sight, he tethered his horse and pulled some food from his saddlebag and waited for night.

Pitch black with barely a moon, he walked back into the quiet town. Admiring the stillness in the dark, he stopped in front of Big Nellie's. He looked up and down the street—almost empty. Empty enough. He took his missive from inside his shirt and unfolded it. He ironed the creases against the building's flat surface. Satisfied, he pulled a small nail from his pocket and his gun from its holster. Using the gun's handle, he pounded the nail into the wood. Again, quite fitting: the gun, same tool used to post their warning, would mercilessly enforce it. He affixed the note for all the Territory to see.

At a more restless pace he returned to his horse, mounted, and rode home through the darkness.

~ ~ ~

In that same pre-dawn dark of Friday, July 26, Cherokee Bill quietly chipped and dug at the grout of the loose bricks in his cell. He neatly piled the grout dust and chips before he removed the brick and saw the revolver and ammunition stored behind. Removing both, he hid them beneath his mattress and then returned the wall to its illusory state of perfection.

~ ~ ~

Getting old, breaking his back in railroad gangs, he'd been waiting for something for thirty years and he didn't have a clue what it was. He'd been waiting like a prisoner, and if he was a prisoner, he was waiting for release with no idea who held the key. Was it the wife who had cursed him and died near 13 years ago, the living child she saddled him with to remind him of her curse, the letter he carried like a lead weight all these years from superstitious fear of what vengeful horrors that dead hag might visit on him if he didn't? Or had he cursed himself? He'd promised that he would rise again and prove the lie of his wife's final accusation—rise from the animal he'd turned into—a transformation born of war and madness, but one that any real woman, any true helpmeet would have eased and assuaged as opposed to inflaming through vicious fishwifery and shrill recriminations. He had been waiting to rise, assuming that ascension would occur as effortlessly and efficiently as had his decline. He had slipped from man to... what he was...to dog... so seamlessly he just knew that the way back would be as easy. So he had waited. He waited. And it had never come. Now his back ached from morning 'til night and his face bore the lines and sunburned mottling of a common cracker that in his former world he would have rightly almost owned; he was indistinguishable from any other man on the railroad line.

His daughter entered the tiny one-room cabin they shared and immediately asked, "How come my Mama didn't leave me nothin'?"

Bill Swain turned and looked at the child as if she had sprouted wings. He jumped from his chair and grabbed her with both hands and shook her.

"Who tol' you to say that?" he shouted. "Who told ya'?"

She shrugged and struggled to free her arms. "Ain't nobody tol' me nothin'. Lemme go."

As he loosened his grip, she said, "I was talkin' to a girl

whose mama died and an' said she lef' her things. Pretty things."

Bill Swain released his daughter.

"I wanted to know if my mama lef' me somethin' like that."

"Your mama didn't leave nobody nothin'," he lied as he slowly returned to his chair, feeling the past's dead hand brush his cheek.

"Will you get me some pretty things?" she said to him with the first vocal and physical undulations of the coquette.

Sickened, Swain rose and slapped her. "You start playin' the whore on me girl an' I will kill you."

She curled her mouth into a snarl as she stormed from the cabin and slammed the door behind her. A few moments later she returned, her face not recovered from the snarl. She marched straight to the pile of dirty blankets in the corner and lay down to sleep. Her father watched her, acknowledging for the first time her age and the promise he carried in his pocket—a promise something inside him would not allow him to ignore, a promise to show the girl the letter with which his dying wife had cursed him. He had promised her, and then he had promised himself. If he could not break the former promise, he had to keep the latter. Watching his girl's face relax into sleep, he saw a threat to even his grossly diminished sense of himself—a diminution he had expected Providence to neutralize as readily as it had conjured it. To date, Providence had disappointed.

This close to Indian Territory, he heard of men with no more than he making prosperous lives for themselves. They gave away land there, and all you had to be was fast enough to get there before all the other crackers with nothing. He could do that. He had been born better. To hell with providence.

He would drag his own self back to worthiness. On July 26, 1895, he decided to cross a border into the notoriously wild Territory.

~

On the morning of the 27th, the sun rose over Okmulgee and, as usual, the proprietor of Big Nellie's place stepped outside his store with a broom in his hand. Sweeping his steps he noticed a piece of paper nailed to his wall. With an inward curse at the vandal who presumed the right to stick it there without so much as a by-your-leave, he ripped it from the wall and discarded it on the pile of dirt, dried horse dung and general debris that he swept out into the street.

Chapters: Natural Selection -- its power compared with man's selection -- its power on characters of trifling importance -- its power at all ages and on both sexes -- On the generality of intercrosses between individuals of the same species -- Circumstances favourable and unfavourable to the results of Natural Selection, namely, intercrossing, isolation, number of individuals -- Slow action -- Extinction caused by Natural Selection -- Action of Natural Selection, through Divergence of Character and Extinction, on the descendants from a common parent -- Low forms preserved -- Summary.

Assaulted by the noise and hurlyburly of St. Louis, Judge Parker longed for and dreaded returning to Ft. Smith's backwards border regions. For a moment, he thought that if he stayed here, in this place that he did not like, for which he had no ambitions, the fate of which was in no way tied to him... if he stayed here, he might not die. Nearing 60, he'd lived longer than many, not as long as some. There was no cosmic injustice in being near death. The doctors he came here to consult expressed sympathy, but no undue surprise. It was not the dying, but the dimming of all things that brought him so low. He was being robbed of his court piece by piece, of his jurisdiction and yes, he acknowledged pride enough to say, his power. His body raged and moaned day and night, bloody piss and his back afflicted so severely that he could sometimes barely move. His life dimmed on all fronts. He knew he should have taken comfort in all that he had accomplished, but he could not. He still did not know what he had hoped for the Territories, but he knew that they had not achieved it. As he prepared to submit himself to God's mercy and judgment, he found himself committing the sin of looking at God's things and finding them wanting. Looking at men, for they were God's one true handiwork, fashioned in His image and so obligated to reflect something of the Godly in their doings. He saw nothing of it there. Were his expectations of God too high for the Almighty to live up to? St. Louis was among the nation's crowning glories. Tall buildings and omnipresent trolley cars, giants of commerce and enormous spiderwebs of wires overhead to service the telegraph and telephone. But he found no more solace here than in Ft. Smith. All of the bustle and flow impressed him no more. He shocked himself as he thought of ants. Virulent, industrious ants hauling boulders from place to place, building hives and gobbling food. It was blasphemous and he chided himself, willfully dismissing the thought as soon as it arrived. But it lingered. So many whom he had spent his days judging and whose deeds he pondered had lied, murdered, raped and stole. At this point, he had to admit that their world had become his. Pitilessly imprisoning them and sentencing them to die, he had virtue on his side, but the trappings with which he had surrounded himself were vice and viciousness. He was more intimately acquainted with the works of murderers than with the works of any other class of men. He had chosen to share their world—on the other side of the line of right; but to think that the stink had not touched him was vanity. The line that had once seemed a chasm was now a little piece of string. In this town full of good, productive men he felt woefully out of place, merely disguised, as if one of them might smell the stench on him and chase him from their midst. He walked along the crowded streets, just another man of business in a summer suit among many almost identical men, but this one steeped in wildness and damnation and he prayed to God to imbue him with the faith of youth wherein man's goodness and preeminence in His eyes (and in his own) was sacrosanct, their works of significance, their lives—his life—of inherent value.

~ ~ ~

Gray smoke filled the prison hallway. Tiny explosions chewed divots in the walls. The deafening gunshot noise magnified the chaos as stinging smoke obscured everything and guards fought scared and belligerent prisoners back into their cells.

It was over. Starr knew it. He didn't know exactly what went wrong but he knew it was over. Bill was trapped. They would kill him. He was probably shooting with a smile on his face—happier than he'd been in a long time. Starr saw a blood-soaked, stiff-backed guard, Larry Keating, proudly, painfully march through the hanging smoke like a dead man and heard him collapse on the ground. Other guards ran to him. Their gunfire died as they dragged him away and then it furiously redoubled as they shot their rage at Bill. Gunpowder burned Starr's nostrils and the omnipresent bullets were like metal rain. Starr couldn't see for the smoke. His ears hurt from the noise and it kept him from thinking things through. First he thought that he didn't want Bill to die and then he threw the thought away because it wasn't his concern—and then another smashing volley from the guards. Why the care for Bill's life? A gunshot pinged off his cell bars sending him deeper into the corner. He didn't want Bill dead. That stayed with him through the noise and gunfire. 'It's a helluva time to learn I like the sonofabitch,' he thought. Cursing himself, he inched low toward his bars and tried to peer through the smoke.

"Bill," he roughly whispered. Then realizing the absurdity of whispering in this inferno, he shouted "BILL!"

"That you Henry?" he heard back.

"Whatchu doin' Bill?"

"Shootin' at folks." Starr had been right. Bill was in high spirits.

"They gonna kill you, Bill." Starr ducked as stray shots grew uncomfortably close. For a moment he feared that Bill might be shooting at him until the wrong wall exploded.

"Ain't dyin'," said Bill. "It's killin'."

The guards stopped shooting. Bill let off a couple of rounds before he realized, then he too stopped. The air still hummed from all the blazing noise. From within the smoky void, a voice called out.

"Bill, this Cap'n Berry. We got men in here an' at least twenty more outside. You ain't gettin' outta here."

"I ain't expectin' to Cap'n," Bill cheerily replied.

"No need for no one else to die is all."

"You gonna keep me alive so you can hang me? Men die from that Cap'n." Three shots burst from Bill's gun.

Henry Starr tore a piece of white from his shirt. Lying on his side he stuck a hand through his cell bars and waved the white rag to get the guards' attention.

"Hey. Hey!" he called hoarsely. He didn't want Bill to hear, but it was too late.

"Whatchu want, Henry?"

Starr took a deep breath. "I wanna talk to the guards."

"Talk fast," Bill replied. "I plan to kill some of 'em."

A guard's rifle shot exploded down the hall. Starr covered his head with both hands.

"Wooo hooo!" Bill cried. "That's what I'm talking'!"

"Cut that out!" Captain Berry hollered at his trigger-happy man. Intrigued by Starr's desire to talk, Berry sent a guard crawling on his belly toward Starr's cell.

"Whatchu got?" the guard whispered as his head pierced the smoke.

"I can get him out," said Starr.

"Bullshit."

"I'll get his gun. But Berry has to promise me—on his word of honor—that he will not shoot Bill when he ain't armed. He's gotta promise on his honor."

"What makes you think he'll come outta there?" The guard ducked lower as Bill's bullets sang overhead.

"He's a friend o' mine," Starr replied. "Go on an' tell Berry," Starr insisted, ignoring the man's dubious looks. The guard disappeared back down the corridor.

Starr crawled to the corner of his cell, thinking what he'd say to convince Bill to surrender. He had no idea. Then, too late, he considered what he should have asked in return. "Damn!" he mumbled smacking a fist on the cell wall. This friendship business did upset a man's priorities, he thought.

The next face Starr saw on the floor near his cell was Captain Berry's. Starr joined him by the bars.

"You get him out," Berry said, "unarmed, and we don't shoot him."

"That's it," Starr said. "And I get somethin', reprieve,

somethin.'"

"I can't do none o' that. Judge Parker's off in St. Louis. I promise to do what I can... a good word for you, what I can, but that's it. You want more we got nothin' to talk about.

Starr didn't have to think about it. "Alright," he said. Berry nodded.

"Bill," Berry called over the din. "This is Captain Berry. All my men hold your fire!" he yelled. The shooting stopped.

"Bill," Berry repeated, audible now.

"Yeah..."

"Got someone wants to talk to you. I'm lettin' him come down there so if you shoot, you're gonna be shootin' him."

"It's Henry, Bill. I'm comin' in."

Silence.

"Whatchu say, Bill?" Henry called.

"Alright."

Berry stood slowly. Equally slowly and looking warily down the hall, he unlocked Starr's cell. He nodded assent and Starr emerged.

"I'm comin' now, Bill," he said with his hands outstretched and visible. "I'm comin'," he repeated.

When he reached Bill's cell, he saw no one. He grasped the bars and swung them open. Walking inside, he found Bill sitting in the corner reloading his revolver. He looked very small hunched down in all the smoke. He looked up at Starr and smiled.

"This plan ain't no good," Bill grinned.

"I said it should o' been Sunday."

Bill finished loading and snapped the barrel shut.

"What they plannin' out there?"

"I think they're shootin' to keep bad Bill from comin' down there and killin' 'em all."

"Bullets flyin' and a jail full o' smoke an' you still full o' shit, Henry."

Starr sat on the cot. Both remained still.

"Ain't heard this in here in a long time," Starr said.

"Nothin'."

"Yep."

The two men looked at each other. Bill cracked a smile.

"I don't know if you're the last face I wanna be seein', Henry."

"Come on out, Bill."

Bill leaned his head back against the wall.

"Whadda you get if I do?"

Starr shrugged. "I don' know."

"But somethin'."

Again, Starr shrugged.

Bill ran his hand across his face, smearing the dark smudges already there. "You doin' this for the love o' Bill?"

"You got one reprieve. Might get another."

"So..."

"It's a chance, Bill."

"They gonna kill me one way or another. I think I like this way."

Starr smiled. "It's awful loud."

Bill had to appreciate that and returned the grin. "I truly thought we'd do it," he said.

"It was a good plan."

"If that goddamn guard o' done what he was tol', we'd be gone."

"I hate a fuckin' hero."

"Shit. What's better 'bout dyin' tomorrow, Henry."

"Not goddamn thing," said Starr. "Jus' ain't today. Jus' not today."

~ ~ ~

Rufus risked going to Okmulgee. He knew the whole place would be humming with his warning to the Territory. That's what he wanted to see—the commotion and the fear he'd engendered. He stole a big hat, pulled it down over his eyes and kept his brown hands in his pockets. With his head hung low, he eyed a growing crowd. His elation faded when he saw that it collected at the wrong store. He looked up the street to Big Nellie's place and no snatch of white hung from the wall. There was such an excitement coming from the growing crowd, though, he moved closer. As he did, he heard the first mutterings.

A thump like a kick to the chest. It skipped a beat, and then his heart raced as if he'd run a mile. Like the jaggedly nauseating smell of skunk the shock stayed in his gut. He gasped in more air as he turned away to be jostled aside by the crowd pushing and scrambling for a closer look at the newsprint dangling in the window. Several simultaneously read aloud from different sections in a chaotic buzz.

He breathed free from the crushing stink of men and women surrounding the posting. It had to be lies. Then he thought of the powers arrayed against men like Bill and himself and yes, he decided, that... yes, this could be. The probability of renewal could be snatched from a brown hand's grasp. He wanted to kill every man and woman in that crowd. In the back of his head, he heard their screams as if in some distant world he acted on his fury—agonies as melodious as psalms. Bill was caught. He had failed and in doing so he might have condemned the Territories to utter usurpation—his people to a particularly cruel and progressive form of enlightened degradation. As high as Bill had flown in his eyes, he sank equally low. He had succumbed. He should not have surrendered. Henry Starr was a liar and a traitor for convincing him to do it. It was—and Rufus literally spat at the thought—the white man in Starr. All the high and mighty words on how the Indians lived and died and he condemns Bill to rot in a cage and die at the end of a white man's rope. Bill had sunk to their level, thinking like them, cowering and mewling for his mere being when all of their blood was at stake. Bill should have died then and there. He killed one guard, but he surrendered. He should have died killing more. There would be no escape and no glory. Not for Bill. Starr would rot in hell. But he, Rufus, could still clean this Territory. It needed to be cleaned—sifted—substance from mush—like horse shit in a pouring rain. His heart still pounded and his head throbbed with the pulse of every beat. But he thought no more of Bill and Starr. Their time had passed. It was his time now.

The murder of Larry Keating on the Friday last in the United States jail has been the theme of conversation on the streets nearly all the week, and the general expression is that the people should have taken Cherokee Bill from the jail and hanged him to a limb, for that is the fate that such hyenas as he deserve. Lynch law is to be deplored in any community, but there are cases where the people are justified in taking the law in their own hands, and this was one of them. The government in this instance demonstrated its inability to properly take care of such men as Cherokee Bill, and the people should have taken the job... and put the monster out of the way forever.

- The Fort Smith Weekly Elevator
August 2, 1895

Betrayed, humiliated, Rufus railed aloud at the cowardly malice of Bill and Henry Starr as he walked the Okmulgee streets. People stared at the sight of the raving boy. He didn't know where he was going and he didn't care until he looked up, shocked on hearing what sounded like his mother's voice. He found himself out back of the mercantile store. From behind a pile of crates he listened.

"John Buck'll be back here an' whatchu gonna do then?"

It was his mother's voice. Rufus peeked from behind the crates and saw Marshal John Garrett towering over her.

"I don't want nothin' from that ol' drunk. I want the boy."

"He's gone," she said.

"Where'd he go?"

"He don't tell. I don't know."

"You in this liquor with him?"

"You mus' be crazy," she scornfully replied.

"If you is, then you owe me the money. You tell him that."

Rufus materialized from behind the barrels. He had his gun in his hand.

A smiling Garrett glanced back and forth between the boy and his mother.

"Shit," he said. "She mus' be in it with you. Put that gun down, boy and gimme my money."

Rufus never glanced at his mother and he never said a word. He stared at a man he hated beyond all others because he was black and did for white ones and did to other black and brown ones.

"You like that Ft. Smith jail, huh?" Garrett taunted, moving forward.

It never occurred to Garrett that Rufus would kill him.

"Gimme my money."

He was just a boy whose Mama stood a few steps away from him.

"You gone dumb, boy?"

Garrett was a United States Marshal in the middle of his own town. It never occurred to him.

Awe marked his face more than pain. He stared at the blood as if he couldn't believe it was his. Rufus shot him again and though his body shuddered, he still did not fall. He barely registered the pain as the metal tore through his flesh. Instead he ogled the boy in disbelief and grudging admiration. He had done what so many had tried and failed to do. One so young—one that he had so misjudged had killed him.

He staggered, and then Rufus shot him a third time.

Rufus' mother gaped as the body hit the ground. She didn't consider her son, only her fear. She didn't move to help the bleeding Marshal. The back door opened and a man peered out. Rufus whipped the gun toward him. The door slammed shut. His mother turned and ran into the store, leaving her son outside with the corpse of the man he had killed.

Hearing the door slam a second time, Rufus looked up and realized his mother was gone. He stood alone in an alley with a bloody, bullet-ridden corpse. He hurried for his horse.

Inside, patrons dared not go near the windows at which they obsessively stared from a safe distance. The man at whom Rufus aimed the gun speechlessly pointed at the door he'd just closed as he warily backed toward the proprietor to warn of the danger. Patrons instinctively backed away as the door opened and Rufus' mother rushed inside, head low, located her husband as if by instinct and pulled him silently toward the exit. He followed without question. They walked in silence to the buggy. He helped her inside and clicked the horse to a trot. Once outside of town, John Buck looked at his wife. The look was a question.

"Rufus killed a man," she said. "A Marshal. Shot him three times."

That was all she said. John Buck said nothing more. Both sat mute at their lack of shock—the strange, longstanding predilection, and now the inexorability. The killing seemed a logical step, an inevitable progression but neither knew from what. Its origin was as vaporous as its fruition was slow. It was back there, both knew, but neither could pinpoint it. They just knew, in hindsight, that it could come.

Rufus galloped back to the gang's camp outside Okmulgee. His speed alerted the others.

"Sam, take it to water," Rufus said handing off his reins. "The rest get the guns, as many as you can... It's started."

7

There had been no scrambling, no haste-fueled clumsiness in the wake of Garrett's murder. Rufus employed the same stride returning to his horse that he had used to leave it. A buzzing marked the difference. It sang in his ears—a monotonous, steady hum as he left the scene. And the passersby, the townspeople... they were different too. Diminished, like the phantoms his parents had become. He might have walked right through one—each so insubstantial a slight wind might have whisked them away.

He paid the ghosts no mind.

Once mounted, he took solace in the horse's graceful, metronomic swaying. For a long while, considering that he had just killed a man, he kept a stately, steady walk—appropriate movement for the singing in his ears—before he spurred to a trot and then a gallop. He rode toward the rolling hills of dried grass dotted with crimped, stunted oaks. The sun-scorched landscape bristled beneath him, as if in anticipation.

At the camp, Lewis, Luckey, Maoma and Sam seemed only slightly more substantial than the people in the town. He quickly told them they had to go. He chafed at their chattering inquiries.

"What's goin' on?

"What happened?

"Bill come?"

Words seemed unnecessary in this world in which he alone had thickness and substance. He used as few as possible to explain that he had killed a Marshal and that Bill had not escaped. As he did, he saw the bullets enter John Garrett's body as if for the first time. The memory felt more real than the actual event. He saw the small spurts of blood from the bullet wound and the look on his mother's face. He saw the finality of the act and the flimsiness of the living flesh he had mangled. Confusingly, he saw both massive import and utter insignificance in Garrett's—in a man's—dying. Which was it? Bill had killed men, as had Henry Starr. For a while, that made them grand in his eyes. He wondered if they had heard the ringing in their ears, as if trapped inside the echo of a church bell's clang? Just a dead colored man—one who'd tried to rob him, but the sound kept on and on, even as the gang's eyes grew wide with excitement at the wonders and horrors that lay ahead of them.

They tripped over themselves frantically scrambling to roll their bedding and saddle their horses while Rufus listened to the relentless screeching in his head. It had marked the killing and the death. Was it the sound of a soul? Did they scream long and loud? Had Callahan been right—was it the creaking hinges of the gates of hell opening up for him... for Garrett?

Just as his gang sat mounted and ready to ride, the screeching stopped. Once more he clearly heard the sounds around him—horse's shod feet tapping on the hard ground, saddles squeaking beneath their riders—no longer as if telegraphed from some great distance. A bird squawked above him and floated boldly—solid and fully alive. The world snapped back from vapor to substance. And now he knew the force of what he'd done and he felt a smile inside. This had not been fantasy or vanity. He was now as deadly as he'd imagined himself; and only deadly men could get things done. His back legs nudged his horse to a lively canter as they headed toward the unknown.

"What we gonna do?" Luckey asked.

"We gonna rob banks?" Lewis chimed in.

"We jus' killed a man," Rufus said as he rode toward the hills, "ain't that enough for one day?"

"We didn't kill nothin'," Maoma groused. "How we know you did?"

"You part o' the Rufus Buck Gang ain't ya'?" Rufus demanded.

"Uh huh."

"You go on back to Okmulgee an' tell 'em that. You'll see what I done."

Maoma rode on in chastened silence.

They camped that night in the wooded hills north of town. As the sun set, Rufus once again basked in the quiet all around him and the sun's vast magic as it disappeared behind green and golden hills. Three young deer stood stock-still on seeing him. He didn't move. He watched them, their fleece-covered racks pointing heavenward. With a bounce the leader leapt into the bushes, the others following. Rufus thought he should have shot one for eating. He'd remember next time.

He didn't want to hide between the trees and hills. He wanted vistas, so he climbed until he looked into the distance without seeing a single man or anything that reeked of one. As the light faded, it was all his, all the green and gold beneath him on all the hills as far as he could see. He held the power of the land, of life and death and he had exercised it as only the chosen and the blessed could. Starr and Sam had failed, but at that moment, he could forgive them, for they had been right. This was what it meant to be free.

~

Next day, a stifling heat settled in. Even in the early morning shadows, warm blasts shunted cool air aside. After a breakfast of dried meat, the gang took to their saddles. Rufus turned east. He was done with the hills. As the trees thinned, the world lay out before him, indelibly beautiful because he knew that he had the power to make it his own. He stopped thinking of rallying Indians to drive whites from the Territory. That was a given. He saw himself as Redeemer. He was Callahan's Moses, imbued with the power to free a land and people. He stopped and stared in gratitude at the magical sight, of which his own eyes might have been the almost-godly source.

Below, he saw some specks moving across the flat land. He kicked his horse to a gallop. Surprised, the others scrambled to keep up.

"What the hell's he doin?" Maoma groused as he steadied himself in his saddle.

The old man did not notice the men riding toward them. His hearing was bad. His daughter touched him and pointed toward the rising dust. Jed Ayers looked behind him, and then from side to side to identify what a group of men would ride so hard toward. He saw nothing. There was no one else. The riders headed straight for him. He had grown old in the Seminole nation, where his daughter had grown to a woman and his wife had died. Like so many others, he had expected great things from these Territories. At the very least, he expected riches. At best, riches with renown. Instead, he had farmed to little end, had dabbled in lumber and cattle to no great result, and had grown old. Now, with his daughter a woman, he did not want her chained to a man like himself—one with great plans in a land that wasn't his because he hadn't the mettle or steel to dream in his own. His few belongings in the wagon, he had left the Seminole nation and crossed the Creek to return to the United States. Of course, he knew of the Territory's outlaws. But he had nothing; he wasn't worth robbing. There were banks and barons aplenty for that.

The Buck gang did not slow until they were right up on the covered wagon. Ayers stopped his horse and waited. His daughter clung to his arm, less in fear than in support. Her main concern was for her father. She planned to see him home, and marry well enough to tend to him for the rest of his life. His disappointments pained her deeply. It was as if he were ill, with cancerous failures and disillusions eating at him. His writhings beneath these ailments were no less aching to her for their lack of physical cause. To her, they deserved no less pity and care.

As the five riders slowed, they circled. Maoma and Sam took the back. Maoma instantly dismounted and dove beneath the wagon's canopy in a gleeful search for treasure. Sam remained seated and fearfully alert. He didn't know what to expect, but with words of Garrett's murder still fresh in his head, he knew it wouldn't be like anything he'd done before.

"Where you comin' from?" Rufus asked the old man.

"Out Wetumka," Ayers replied.

"That's Seminole Nation."

Ayers shook his head in assent.

"You ain't Seminole."

Lewis giggled, but stifled the sound when no one joined him. They all heard Maoma's rattling and banging from the back of the wagon. Ayers turned to look, but his daughter tightened her grip on his arm, and he thought better of it.

"Where you headed?"

"Home."

"Should o' never left."

"I know that," Ayers testily replied. "I don't need some boy to tell me that."

"We just want to go back to West Virginia," his daughter interrupted. "We're just going home."

"This is the Rufus Buck Gang. I'm Rufus Buck. I killed a man yesterday and I ain't no boy."

Rufus slid from his saddle and eyed the shaking, rattling wagon.

"What they got in there?" Rufus yelled.

Maoma jumped down holding a lady's corset against his chest, mincingly mimicking coquettish ways.

"What they got!" Rufus demanded.

Disappointed at the reaction to his antics, Maoma let the garment fall.

"Ain't got shit," he said.

"We are poor people," the daughter pleaded. "Please, just let us go home."

"You been a white man in Seminole and you ain't got

nothing?"

Ayers knew this final mocking to be richly deserved, and it had extra sting coming from the mouth of an Indian. He hovered between fury and self-pity. He brandished his whip and snapped his reins to run for it. His horse jerked forward and the big wagon shuddered.

"Whoa!" Rufus shouted, grabbing the horse's bridle. "Get 'em down," he shouted at his men. Luckey grabbed the woman and hauled her roughly from the wagon. Lewis did the same for the man, practically carrying him like a child as he struggled.

Rufus pointed his gun at them. Sam slowly slipped from his saddle. Maoma immediately drew his own gun. Sam reached for his, but settled for resting his palm on the handle.

"Should o' left a long time ago," Rufus repeated. He saw something of his father's look in the old man. A white man with nothing, he realized, looked a lot like an Indian with everything taken from him.

"Please," the woman said. "We won't say anything. We'll just get in the wagon and go."

"We want you to say somethin'," Rufus replied. "That's the whole point. You got to have somethin' to say."

Maoma walked up to the woman and put his hand on her breast. The father lurched at him and Sam easily held him back.

"Let me at her," Maoma said.

Rufus still had the bridle in his hand. He turned his attention to the horse. He stroked its nose and petted its neck, allaying its fear. Correctly taking the cue, Maoma dragged the woman from Luckey's grasp and rushed her to the other side of the wagon. She did not scream as she was yanked away, though tears fell down her face.

Shocked at his sudden empty-handedness, Luckey followed. Left holding the old man, and seeing all the others rushing after Maoma, Sam dragged the old man in the same direction.

"You should o' left," Rufus shouted after them. He did not move from the horse's side. He did not stop petting it. He smiled when it lowered its head and snorted, signaling its comfort. Rufus expected to hear a woman's screams, but he did not.

"Get your filthy hands offa her!" he heard Ayers shout. "I'll kill you," the old man wept hysterically.

The old man reminded him of his Daddy, but if men like him hadn't come to the Territory, maybe his Daddy wouldn't be like he was. Old or not, poor or not, he had to learn.

The old man did not speak again. No one spoke. Rufus heard a few whimpers, one high pitched with pain—from a woman—and a few groans from his men.

"Hold him," he finally heard. It was Lewis. Rufus wondered if the old man watched. He knew his father would have watched. It would have made the pain all the more indelible, as if he'd learned to live on it like most men live on food. He bet the old man watched.

A couple of minutes later, Maoma appeared. The others followed him. Maoma was the only one who smiled, but even his smile was furtive. The others looked guiltily toward the ground. None looked at Rufus. He tried to meet the eyes of each, but only got surreptitious glances.

He left the horse and crossed to the other side of the wagon. There he saw the woman, dirty and bedraggled, as she helped her limp father up from the ground. The old man shook his head from side to side repeating, "no no no no no no no," again and again. That's all he did.

Rufus instinctively moved to help, but the woman cast him a contemptuous glance that repelled him like a blow. In that glance was every man and woman who had looked at him like he was dirt. In it was all the contempt that the Territory's white men heaped upon his father and his mother. It was the look that made Cherokee Bill shoot a man for simply eyeing him. He grabbed her hair and jerked her face toward his and spat in it. For the first time, he saw real fear in her eyes and for the first time in this encounter he felt good. He threw her to the ground and walked away. He was furious that he had almost wasted a kind gesture on her.

Standing in a huddle, Lewis, Luckey, Maoma and Sam stopped talking when Rufus reappeared. They watched him, assuming that he had partaken as they had. They looked for a sign that it was true, but saw only anger. They knew what they had done to a woman and all their lives they'd heard that it was wrong, but still they thought they should celebrate. They were outlaws and this is what outlaws did. They didn't know how to respond. Should they feel proud? Redeemed? Had it been right, or wrong?

They watched as Rufus climbed on his horse and headed east. They kept hoping for his blessing on their venture. But he gave them nothing. Silently they followed, dissatisfied, as if they'd been robbed of a joy that was their due. There should have been a celebration. Maoma would have liked to further ransack, and perhaps even burn the wagon. Luckey and Lewis had, during Rufus' absence, briefly wondered what money or other wealth the old man might have hidden. They had hoped for a chance to find it. Riding along behind their glum, silent leader, the boys felt dutiful, not free. They looked forward to the next encounter—which they felt sure would be more satisfying.

Rufus' anger did not abate. The rebuff from the old man's daughter slashed at him like a whip.

Later that day, heading toward Berryhill Creek, they spotted a lone white man on horseback. The four gang members waited, almost breathless, desperate to unleash the euphoric geyser Rufus had artificially capped during the Ayers encounter.

Without a sign or signal, Rufus galloped. Mouths and eyes widened in glee as the gang whooped and dust flew beneath the horses' hooves. Seeing the horses barreling toward him, the lone rider tried to run, but his horse was no match for the Rufus Buck Gang. He stopped when they passed him, cocooned in dust as the five riders circled. He raised his hands in submission.

"My name is Jim Shafey," he said loudly, as the horses slowed around him. "I ain't armed. I got no gun. You can take what money I got."

Rufus pulled his Winchester from its saddle holster.

"Oh please God no," Shafey pled as the barrel pointed at him.

Rufus swung the gun around and used the butt to knock him from his horse.

"Clean him out, boys," Rufus sang.

The gang swarmed on him—turned out every pocket,

removing his boots, and touching every inch of his body as if exulting in their ability to do so.

"Don't forget the horse," Rufus called.

Lewis abandoned Shafey and rifled the saddlebags.

Maoma backed away from the melee fondling a gold watch. He could tell it was real gold. No one could have told him different. He'd never touched gold; never seen it. Luckey and Sam stood counting fistfuls of crumpled bills.

"You know this is Indian Territory," Rufus said.

"I'm a walnut log man. This is logging country."

"You ain't Indian. You ain't got the sense to know you don't belong someplace called 'Indian Territory' when you ain't Indian?"

Shafey didn't know what to say. "This is good logging country," he repeated helplessly.

"Take his clothes off him."

"I got his boots already," Maoma announced as he dove at Shafey. They took his belt, his pants and his shirt. Moama ripped his drawers off of him. They left him his socks.

"Whoo hoo, look at that little thing he got," Maoma hollered.

"Get out," Rufus said to Shafey. "Any blood you leave behind is pay for what you took."

"Cut him up," said the usually silent Sam as he stared at the naked white man. "Kill him."

Sam's outburst amazed them, as did the malicious snarl he wore. During the ensuing, shocked silence, though, his words came to seem like sanction.

Pleased for the first time since he killed Marshal Garrett, Rufus slid from his saddle. He traded his rifle for a knife. He approached Shafey. He touched the hairy white skin as you would an animal's—as you would something curious and alien. Then he slid his sharp knife across it. The skin opened like a flower and blood oozed. Shafey gasped at the initial sting and grimaced at the growing pain. He turned to run but careened into Sam who grabbed his arms. Maoma and Luckey pointed their revolvers at him.

"You gonna kill him?" Lewis asked softly, unable to mask his unease.

Luckey lowered his gun as if in deference to his big friend's disquiet. Rufus looked again at the bleeding, naked white man amongst them, so dissonant, like a gasping fish in the treetops.

"Okay," Rufus decided. "We'll vote. Who says we kill him?"

Sam and Maoma flung their hands in the air.

"Who says we don't?"

Lewis slowly raised his hand. Luckey followed.

Rufus made a show of examining Shafey. He looked him up and down, walked a thoughtful circle around him. He lifted Shafey's penis with his knife. Shafey gasped at the gesture.

Rufus set the knife edge, already wet with blood, against the white man's stomach and pulled it slowly against the skin, digging deeper and pushing harder until his knife point disappeared deep into the soft flesh. The skin and the muscle beneath split like cloth. Blood poured down his nakedness. Shafey's mouth opened in mute agony.

"We keep him alive," Rufus said. "Like the others. So he can tell." He pointed the knife at Shafey.

"What Territory is this?" Rufus asked as the blood wept down the white skin and the wound gaped like a hungry mouth.

"Indian Territory," Shafey gasped.

"Who don't belong here?"

"I don't belong."

Rufus slashed the knife across Shafey back. He screamed.

"What you gonna tell other folks like you?"

"They don't belong."

He hacked the blade's edge into Shafey's thigh as if he were chopping wood. He had to yank to pull the knife free. Howling, Shafey fell. Sam let him.

"Tell 'em it's the Rufus Buck Gang," were the last words Shafey heard.

Bill Swain did not look toward the hills. He needed food and he needed work to get it. That's all he thought about. He didn't know how far Okmulgee was, but from the last set of directions, he planned to get there by nightfall.

Because he did not look toward the hills, he did not see them coming.

About a half a mile behind her father's wagon, Theodosia saw the dust cloud. She imagined it heralded magic and ghosts. Spotting horses' flying manes and sweat-shiny coats, she was satisfied. They looked like nothing she had ever seen. She'd never seen them pushed so hard, their mouths open and their hooves whipping toward her in a pounding blur. She stopped and watched as they neared her father's wagon.

The gang had a template for taking lone travelers. They descended at breakneck speed and didn't slow until they had run their prey to ground. Bill Swain found himself surrounded by steaming horses and brown men. The very sight of them incited fury.

"What the fuck you want?" he demanded.

As the men surrounded her father's wagon, Theodosia watchfully strolled toward them. She saw three guns pointed at her father. She saw his anger. She liked what she saw.

"I ain't got shit," Bill Swain raged. "I ain't got food to eat so it's a fool who tries to rob me."

"What you doin' in Indian Territory?" Rufus calmly asked.

"What the fuck is it to you?"

"It's my land. We the Rufus Buck Gang."

"I don't care if you Jesus goddamned Christ, I still ain't got shit an' you can just get on."

Rufus noticed the approaching young girl. The gun fell from his hand. The panicked Maoma dove spectacularly from his horse to recover it. Rufus gaped, open mouthed, as if witnessing the unimaginable. All eyes followed his to rest on Theodosia. Her blonde hair, even dulled with dirt and grease, shimmered yellow and gold. Barefoot, her dirty dress barely fell to her knees as she concentrated all of her attentions on using one foot and then another to roll a rounded rock ahead of her. She seemed to have forgotten the men with guns.

Rufus jumped from his horse and watched as she came closer, expecting the heat to shimmer and wash her away. But she came closer and she was real. He recognized her—from her hair to her skin, from her mouth to her unbelievably light brown eyes—it was her, covered in the Territory's dust and dirt as if the earth itself had thrown her up. It was his Angel.

When she reached the wagon, she abruptly raised her head and carefully regarded each of them, one by one, as if expertly examining goods for barter.

"What they want, Pa?" she asked innocently as her eyes fixed on Rufus.

"Money," he replied. "All any bunch o' niggers and injuns want and what I ain't got.

"Shut up," Rufus said to Swain, eyes on the magic girl as Maoma literally placed the gun back in his hand and, scared that it would fall again, closed Rufus' fingers around it.

"What you mean, shut up..."

Rufus blindly shot his gun in Swain's direction, his eyes

never leaving Theodosia, who grinned as her father ducked and covered his head as she had done so many times before. Rufus smiled back at her. He had recognized his Angel, and now, she had acknowledged him.

"I know you," he said.

"I ain't seen you before," she replied, swaying from side to side. "You shot at my Daddy."

"I didn't hurt him."

"Could you?"

"If I wanted."

She looked at her father.

"I saw you in a dream," Rufus cooed.

"Was my Daddy in your dreams?" she asked.

"Girl, get up here!" Swain yelled.

She waltzed slowly toward Rufus. She reached out and picked up his arm. She examined his hand as she would an odd piece of stone. "You're a nigger," she said softly.

"I'm Creek, too," he replied.

"My Daddy hates niggers." She stroked the brown skin on Rufus' hand as if it were velvet.

"Goddammit girl you get away from him. Get up here!"

She glanced at her father with a newfound dispassion that bordered contempt.

"You all outlaws, huh?"

Rufus nodded assent. "The Rufus Buck Gang."

"What you all do?"

"We drive white folks outta Indian Territory."

"HA!" Bill Swain spat.

Rufus aimed his gun at Bill Swain's head.

"We'll do it like this," Rufus said. "I start shootin' at five.

One... two..."

"C'mon girl!" Swain yelled at Theodosia.

She looked at her father as if he were no one.

"...three..."

"Holy God, fuck dammit!" Swain frantically snapped his reins. His mare hurried forward.

"We didn't rob him," Maoma complained.

"We ain't got nothin'" Theodosia assured, and then smiled. She turned to Rufus.

"I'm white," she said.

"You started it," Rufus said, eying her like a prize. "Weren't for you, wouldn't be no Buck Gang. You ain't white," he told her. "You more 'n that. Whiter 'n white."

She beamed. Her teeth flashed between her full, pink lips. She took his hand, clasped it, and playfully swung it back and forth. Rufus too smiled as she followed him to his horse. He mounted, and then dragged her up behind him. His skin tingled as she put her hands around his waist. Grabbing the reins, his hand touched the flesh of her smooth thigh and it was as warm and soft as in his dream.

Luckey and Lewis wordlessly expressed their awe at the audacity of taking a white girl so quickly. Sam and Maoma sat taller in their saddles.

News of the white woman's rape at the hands of five colored fiends paralyzed Okmulgee—along with news of the old man forced to watch his daughter so befouled—and then the tale of the naked and hacked up Jack Shafey stunned the town.

According to the newspapers, during the course of her repeated ravishments, the woman received critical injuries. The man, they said, was so disfigured by knife wounds that he would never be able to show his face again. Soon everyone knew whom to blame. The name Rufus Buck bounced off the walls of every home where every man feared for the virtue of his wife and his daughters. Buck's unspeakable deeds and unthinkable motive of eradicating those who would make something out of this rough, naked land ignited every telegraph wire, precluding sleep, rattling dreams, and worst of all, kindling fears of a battle against an enemy on his own land and full of such righteous zealotry and vengeful brutality—a battle that, should the Indians of the Territories rise up and follow, not even white men squatting on Indian land would know for sure they had the right to win.

Throughout his preparations for the Buck trial—the formulation of the lies and obfuscations increasingly necessary to feed the illusions he required to make it through each day—phrases from the book lashed out at him like serpents. Reading bone-dry descriptions of natural phenomena, words suddenly assaulted him as if usurped and perverted by a merciless Evil.

> *Hence, as more individuals are produced than can possibly survive, there must in every case be a struggle for existence, either one individual with another of the same species, or with the individuals of distinct species, or with the physical conditions of life.*

So he read the whole as if navigating a minefield, heart pounding, nerves spent, knowledge that the next words might strike. He tried to understand. It was like a code, foul profundities hidden in seemingly benign and sympathetic prose.

> *... we need feel no surprise at the inhabitants of any one country, although on the ordinary view supposed to have been specially created and adapted for that country, being beaten and supplanted by the naturalised productions from another land. Nor ought we to marvel if all the contrivances in nature be not, as far as we can judge, absolutely perfect; and if some of them be abhorrent to our ideas of fitness.*

Aberrations, legions of them, perhaps chosen by the mute earth itself as most fit to inhabit it. An earth contemptuous of virtue, and ignorant of the resurrection of the body of Our Lord.

> *We need not marvel at the sting of the bee causing the bee's own death; at drones being produced in such vast numbers for one single act, and being then slaughtered by their sterile sisters; at the astonishing waste of pollen by our fir-trees; at the instinctive hatred of the queen bee for her own fertile daughters; at ichneumonidae feeding within the live bodies of caterpillars; and at other such cases. The wonder indeed is, on the theory of natural selection, that more cases of the want of absolute perfection have not been observed.*

Rufus Buck had killed John Garrett. He was one such aberration. The girl, with her white skin and beauty, even more so. The soul he'd sought to save in Buck had committed the sin of cold-blooded murder. Buck was not the first of his inmates to commit another crime. But Parker had distinguished this one with particular attention. On this one he had wagered the value of his stewardship of the Territories. Was he doing God's work? Buck would tell. Redeeming the son to assuage John Buck, the father, was to have been the justification for his reign over the Territories—the particular to represent the whole.

When he began, he had thought God guided his hand. But that balm had abandoned him and he could not sufficiently trace his steps to discover where he had lost his way and perhaps regain His path. Since he could no longer think his work Divine in origin, he could no longer whitewash its viciousness to some, and its failure to rise to the standards he had dreamt for it. But he could make amends. If John Buck had been the victim of his stewardship, Rufus Buck would reap the reward. On the day of Rufus Buck's sentence for the paltry crime of whiskey peddling, he had taken responsibility for him just as he had taken responsibility for the Territories all those years ago. Acceding to the failure of his Territorial dominion—the collapse of his Lordly experiment with living men—he planned to redeem himself through this one boy. His grand Territorial whole may have turned dubious or even monstrous, he thought, but he could make this small, purely human amends.

When he heard about John Garrett's murder, a cold tingle settled on him. Shot three times in an alley. The Rufus Buck he had saved. An abrupt turn, a descent. Wrongness and no control. And then he'd learned the true tale of that monstrous little girl—a white girl so young, who should have been so innocent. He felt a perilous unraveling of the fabric he had woven in this land, and worse, he realized that the order he had placed upon it was not only Godless, but illusory—a sheer linen mocking a woolen blanket.

He felt powerless, which compelled him back to Virgil Purefoy's damnable book.

The whole of it was insidious. He sensed it, though he could not fully comprehend it. He paused in his reading to absorb outrageous passages, to reread them and let his mind accept the alien concepts, like wood does a stickpin under pressure. He snatched moments of understanding, but they made the whole more terrifying. He read compulsively—every line, some more times than he could count. Signs, symbols. Vague hints of shocking import. A riddle and a trick. Talk of low things—butterflies and zebras, their habitats and morphology, interspersed with missiles of blasphemy sharp enough to pierce his mind. He damned himself for slurping it up like the most sinful glutton, but he could not stop. He sensed truth in it. That was his sin. That was his curse.

When he first learned the extent of Buck's malice, he feared his chest would crack from the effort of breathing. He had not heard the knock, but saw Bass Reeves' face in his doorway. His principal Marshal wore an unaccustomed look. Parker saw fear on the face that had never shown any.

"Judge, there's trouble."

Parker gave the Marshal his full attention.

"There's been a rape, and a... cutting." Reeves struggled for the words to describe it. Then he blurted, "They made her Daddy watch! Then they cut a man all up an' left him nothing, not a stitch on his back."

"Who?" Parker asked as he rose.

"They said the Rufus Buck Gang."

That's when Parker fell to his knees. He collapsed as if hands slammed down on his shoulders to force him into this sinfully alien position of submission and humility. The force exerted was so physically powerful that he actively resisted the urge to fold his hands and pray for mercy—to pray that no deeper supplication be demanded of him. Reeves ran to drag him to a chair.

"Lemme get help," Reeves said, already halfway to the door.

"No!" Parker insisted. "Just water. Just water. Please."

Reluctantly, Reeves complied. As Parker reached for the water, Reeves could not miss his trembling hand, so he placed his own on top of Parker's to support the glass. After a deep draught, Parker breathed easier, and smiled, waving Reeves and the water away.

"When did this happen?" he asked.

"Both two days ago."

"Nothing since?"

"Not that we know. Buck was talkin' about white folks in the Territory. He told em' all to get out, and to tell all the rest to go, too, or face the same."

"He killed John Garrett, and now this," Parker muttered to himself. "How is the woman?"

"She's strong, Judge. Tol' us all she could. She wants to go mighty bad, though. They was on their way back home, Virginia I think."

"Bring them to me. The woman and her father and the other man. If they can't come here, I will go to them. I need to hear them. I need to see."

"Yes sir."

"Capturing the Buck Gang is your priority."

"No different than after Garrett," Reeves replied. "Only now we're lookin' for five of 'em."

Reeves nodded and turned to the door. "You sure you don't want me to get you someone?" he asked the judge.

"No. Thank you."

One of his deputies had been murdered in broad daylight and cold blood. A woman had been raped and her father forced to watch. Another man had been, from all descriptions, mutilated. He had meant to save Buck, to erase the accusatory image of so many like his shattered father—by saving the son. He had sought to salve his conscious for the damage he had done, facilitated, and acceded to, and now he would pay for seeking cheap redemption for crimes so intractable that any Christian would have known there could be no forgiveness. God would only sink him further as punishment for his ghastly hubris.

Now he would hear it all. He would minister to the victims and absorb their tales and horrors—with the knowledge that they, among so many others, lay on his head.

~

It was news about the Buck Gang that drove him to Cherokee Bill's cell that day.

"What did he want?" he had asked the murderous half-Indian.

"To make things like they was before," Bill replied. "For the

Indians."

To turn back to a time he could only imagine. Fantasy. He wanted what any boy wants, only he had the spleen and steel to grab for it at any cost. He saw similar in Bill—a child, clutching at things, grasping at and throwing things, doing untold damage to satisfy his wants and leaving blood and wreckage in his wake.

He fought for ways to distinguish himself and his acts from Bill's. He had not known. He had sought only to do good and God's will—and not from greed or covetousness. He could not have known what the book said—that some deviations of structure so strongly pronounced as to deserve to be called monstrosities arise, or that we forget that the birds which are idly singing around us mostly live on insects or seeds, and are thus constantly destroying life or that improving the stock in a particular place is done with equal efficacy, though more slowly, by nature, in the formation of varieties of mankind, fitted for the country which they inhabit. He had forgotten the country he inhabited. He had thought it close to heaven, had dreamed that he could make it so. In fact, it might have been a form of hell.

Bill broke men and so did Buck. They shot and hacked and raped them. Parker broke a land and its peoples. The white ones trampled everything in their wake and the brown ones either slunk beneath the onslaught or hacked away at everything without conscience. Both were products of this place. Both were his doing. He sought Bill and felt pity for Buck because he and they were one. It was all of them—all of the "great" men desperate to change their worlds. They were grasping children, doing untold damage to satisfy wants they arrogantly attributed to God and higher callings, and leaving behind them little more than ghastly tales and vaguely remembered tears.

~ ~ ~

Theodosia liked the warmth. Despite the heat, she pressed herself against Rufus Buck as she clasped his waist. Through her thin dress she felt his body heat and the contours of his skin—the undulation of his ribs, his stomach, his chest. She laid her cheek against his back and faintly heard his heartbeat. She had rarely felt a human touch. Her father did not hoist her aloft or affectionately chafe her. He did not hug or hold her. He had only even hit her a few times, but sufficiently hard that she learned her lesson and he didn't have to do it often. She had no other kin. She was an island, but made of flesh, as if set apart from other men and women by an invisible sea. She saw them holding hands on the street, cradling young ones, leading them by the hand, children climbing atop one another like puppies, but none of that happened to her. No one touched or cradled or fondled her. She did not know why. She figured she was different. Dangerous, like the flesh-rending, scavenging animals she compulsively spied on. Like the big black birds she so loved to watch. These dark ones, too, were different—swooping down on their wagon as no one ever had, defying her father as she had never considered, whisking her up and flying her away as if she were a mouse in a field. She had always watched and wondered at the black and brown ones in the towns they passed. Her father didn't treat them like he did the white ones. He treated them like they were nothing. He treated them like he treated her. She hadn't dared, but she wanted to approach them, to see if, secretly, behind the skin, she was like them and that was why none of the white ones would touch her. She thought of asking her father if that's why they wandered, why they never settled down or grew to know places or people; but with his teeth gnashing and grumbling about "niggers" when he encountered the dark ones, she figured she'd better not. He hated them, so she didn't want to ask if she and her father were like them, though she suspected. Now, as she thrilled to the horse galloping beneath her and held onto the man who had snatched her away from the wagon she'd followed all her life like a mule, as she closed her mouth against the flying bugs, felt their tiny sting as they smashed against her face, as the earth sailed beneath her as if she were not of it, for the first time in her life she knew that she was where she ought to be. For the first time she knew that she was free and she belonged.

She and Rufus did not speak during that first brisk ride. Feeling her arms tight around him, looking down and seeing her soft, white hands, he rode with a resoluteness he had always sought, but never known—with an Angel on his back, her wings outspread, flying across the world. He squinted against the wind and absorbed its urgency. It spurred him with sultry, silent encouragements that dangled all the wonders he could achieve before him like jewels. He knew his destination, and knew its fatefulness to be Divine in its justice. Benton Callahan, a cattleman who grazed his herds on Indian

Territory, was the son of H.P. Callahan, who had called him filth and expelled him from the Wealaka Mission school with a venomous, spittle-filled torrent of revulsion and disgust... Benton Callahan, son of H.P. Callahan, had a ranch southeast of Okmulgee. That's where Rufus rode.

~

His first shot hit the colored cowboy's horse. It's legs buckled beneath it and the cowboy flew from his saddle like a cannon ball. Grazing cattle bolted to a cacophony of mooing and thumping hooves. Slowly, the ground began to shake beneath the heavy animals' rumblings. Wide-eyed Theodosia panted with excitement. Rufus leapt from his horse and marched toward Benton Callahan, who, recovering nearby from the shock of seeing his man shot down, spurred his horse. A bullet ripped through the horse's back leg and Callahan hit the ground. The black cowboy got back to his feet and tried to run. Sam and Maoma both fired wildly at him. Blood sprayed from the cowboy's shoulder and he pitched forward yet again. He didn't move this time. Two horses thrashed and screamed wildly in pain. Callahan crab-walked backwards away from the gang, terror in his eyes. With the black cowboy laying bloody and still, Sam and Maoma turned their guns to Callahan. Shots popped and he felt a furious burning, as if the side of his head were on fire. When he lowered his hand from the burning, the hand dripped blood. Lewis shot one horse in the head, silencing it, and then shot the other.

Theodosia bounced up and down, unable to contain her excitement. Her head shook as if she couldn't decide in which thrilling direction to look. Her arms slapped at her sides and her feet shuffled like her breathlessly indecisive eyes. She half giggled while gasping air as if there were not enough in the world to sate her.

Luckey stood over the black cowboy lying face-down on the ground, the top of his shirt now soaked with blood. Luckey hesitantly nudged the body with his foot. The cowboy didn't budge.

"Is he dead?" Luckey asked.

Lewis shrugged. "Dunno," he replied.

Rufus stood over the bleeding Callahan, "Your Daddy tell you 'bout me?"

Still scooting away on his backside, he vigorously shook his bloody head from side to side.

"He threw me outta his school," Rufus continued, brandishing his gun as carelessly as you would a stick. "Called me all kinda names. I had a knife. Should o' stuck him."

"I'm sorry," Callahan mumbled, trying to keep his eyes on all the gang at once.

"You gonna shoot him?" Theodosia excitedly screeched her arms circling and feet hopping as if skipping an invisible rope.

"I don' know."

She moved closer. "I think you shot his ear off."

"I didn't shoot him. Musta been Maoma."

"Lemme see," she said to Callahan, approaching him. His hand remained glued to his bleeding head. "I wanna see it. I wanna see what's left."

She gingerly touched his stubborn hand, as if it had thorns, and quickly pulled away. With a look of supreme confusion, he stared from man to man for answers, desperately questioning this little white girl's presence and participation; but he got no answers, which only deepened his confusion and fear. Impatient, she slapped at his hand, trying to knock it away, but still as smartly as if it might bite back.

"I wanna see," she demanded.

Rufus raised his gun. "Show her," he ordered. "Your Daddy cut some blood on me with his little whip. Now the Rufus Buck gang's got some o' yours."

"I got nothin' to do wit' my Daddy," Callahan pleaded.

"My Mama said that the son lives with what the Daddy does, and his Daddy before. That's why Indians got nothin'."

"Please," Callahan almost wept. "What do you want? Take anything."

"I wanna see his ear!" Theodosia shouted.

Rufus flicked the gun at Callahan's hand. It slowly fell from his head. Theodosia's face glowed with expectation. She stooped down next to the head, and peered at the red, pulpy mass that hung from the side of his face where his ear used to be. She reached out with her finger and quickly touched it. As the loose flesh jiggled, she snapped her hand away as if toying with sparks. Callahan screamed. Her eyes and feet danced again at the correlation: her touch and his scream. Quickly, surreptitiously, as if petting a snake, she touched it again, and again, the big man screaming and flinching each time, sitting with his arms across his chest, as if to keep his body from falling apart, moans and yowls accompanying the tears streaming down his face.

"I ain't never seen what's inside a ear," Theodosia announced as she turned away.

"He dead now?" Luckey asked Lewis as Theodosia skipped

toward the black cowboy lying on the ground. Lewis dutifully kicked the body once more. The test was, again, inconclusive.

The girl approached and scrutinized the body with the big red stain. She struggled to turn it over. That done, she dipped her hand in the blood and felt the wound. After chasing the gang members with her reddened hand, she found nothing more of interest there.

"We gonna shoot him?" Maoma asked of Callahan.

Rufus regarded at the weeping cattleman. He imagined his former teacher's reaction upon hearing of this day. He imagined the father suffering by proxy the son's humiliation.

"No. Take what you want. He's gonna wear that face forever. His Daddy's gonna look at it until he dies and know it was his doin', and me who done it."

With a growing rage, Rufus grabbed Callahan by the hair and jerked his head up. "He shouldn't o' said those things," Rufus spat at S.P. Callahan's son. "He shouldn't o' done it."

9

"I saw you in a dream," he said to the wandering girl who paced, hopped, and strolled from one spot of nowhere-in-particular to another in blissful self-involvement as if practicing intricate dance steps. Rufus wasn't sure if she heard him. He looked up. The glowing, fiery sunset screamed the earth's own satisfaction at his work. Burnt orange and crimson, the colors seeped like blood across the sky. He had ridden with his Angel's arms around him.

"Like when you wake up screamin' at night?" she asked, eyes fixed on her ever-moving feet and the dry, cracked ground they covered.

"Not nightmares," Rufus corrected. "Good dreams."

"My Daddy has the bad ones."

"It was an Angel," he said. She stopped her strange dancing and looked at him.

"Like in heaven?" she asked, her in a scowl of disbelief.

"Uh huh."

She giggled. "But I ain't dead." She lifted her arms from her sides and began her jagged dance again. "I don't think so."

Rufus shrugged. "Maybe it wasn't you. Maybe it was a sign, and the Angel made herself look like you 'cause she knew

I'd find you."

"What'd she say?"

"That I had to drive the white folks outta the Indian Territory."

"How come?"

"It's how it was. How it's supposed to be."

"My Daddy woulda been glad you shot a nigger today. My Daddy hates niggers."

"Well I hate white people."

"I'm white."

"You're the Angel."

"Angels is white." Her previously elaborate movements devolved into an imaginary game of hopscotch.

Rufus watched the darkness grow all around him.

"If you hate 'em, how come you didn't shoot the white one, too?"

Rufus shrugged. "So he'll go tell all the rest that they gotta leave."

"My Daddy ain't leavin'. They gonna kill you."

"Not if I kill them first."

"Then you better start killin'.

"I killed a man jus' yesterday!" Rufus insisted.

She placed one foot precisely before the other as if walking a tightrope. "Prob'ly just another nigger."

They camped not far from John Buck's ranch. After the day's blood and frenzy, the place had tugged at Rufus and he had followed. It was safe. Rufus was far enough from his father's to keep the old man out of danger, and close enough to enjoy his proximity—to know and exploit the terrain.

Maoma and Sam excitedly relived the day's mayhem, reenacting scenes and taking turns playing outlaw and victim. Lewis and Luckey were sufficiently removed from memories of flies buzzing on the dead and near-dead, anguished horses screaming, from the eerie stillness amidst the quickly browning blood—far enough from the sights and sounds to concentrate not on the disquieting aspects of corpses and killing, but on the excitement of galloping down from the hills on unsuspecting men—white men—who cowered before them—of themselves as the most powerful force as far as they could see. They lay on their blankets, luxuriating in it.

Theodosia discovered a new world that day, like walking inside a magnificent dollhouse. Everything changed. The air, the light, her self, her company and what she was in the world. She had changed. She had become one of the big, black birds she'd always admired for their ravaging efficiency. All of her life people from town to town had floated past her as if imported from a different kind of life than she could ever know, like different beings—observed as if from a lowly backstage seat. Now she stripped them from the world like the birds stripped flesh from the corpse—so much more liberating a role than a mouse in the corner, a silent watcher forever apart. Her arms flapped slowly and leaned forward to see if the wind would take her.

As she bent forward, Rufus leapt from the ground and grabbed her around the waist. He rubbed his stiff penis against her buttocks as he raised her thin dress.

"Cut it OUT!" she screamed as she pounded at the hands that held her waist so tight she could barely move.

His fingers yanked down her threadbare drawers. Sparse hair, a cleave, and then warm moisture encased his exploring fingers. Theodosia convulsed. She uttered a concussive grunt, as if kicked in the gut. Her struggling stopped. His fingers sank insider her and moved in and out as his hand tugged and pulled and rubbed, smearing her wetness all over her down there. Her eyes wide, she marveled at the intermittent shudders, the chills that cut right down inside her. He'd move his hand and there it was and she'd grunt and sigh like an animal. She pushed her middle into is hand wanting more. He dragged her drawers down to her feet and fumbled with his own belt. He pushed her head down and then she felt like she'd been stabbed. She screamed. The shudders were gone—just gasping pain. He pushed hard against her again and again and each time it felt like she was torn apart. She tried to straighten but his strong hand held her head down. She tried to walk forward, but he tottered right behind, still pushing his penis inside her. He began to moan more and more loudly. She grabbed the hand not holding her down and sank her teeth into his arm. The flesh gave way and she tasted his blood in her mouth. Rufus screamed as his body shivered and he grasped her even more tightly against his exploding orgasm. He drew backwards and pushed her away. She fell to the ground and he to his knees, cradling his bleeding arm.

Maoma, Sam, Luckey and Lewis stood behind a wild hedge, watching Rufus and Theodosia, each stroking his penis, each heavy-lidded and dreamy as hands pumped madly and synchronous thick splats of ejaculate soared like white fireworks into the air before them.

"Goddammit whadja do that for!?" Rufus cried, cradling his bloody arm.

"Me?" Theodosia screamed back. "What'd you do!?"

"I was lovin' you!"

She rose, rushed at him and kicked him. "That hurt like hell," she screamed.

"It's what men and women do."

"If they tryin' to kill each other." She moaned in pain and doubled over, clutching her blood-stained dress against her crotch.

Rufus realized her pain was real. He walked to her and tenderly placed his hand on her shoulder. "I'm sorry," he said.

She jerked his hand away.

"It sounded like you was likin' it," he pleaded.

She pouted. "At first. A little. Then you started cuttin' me up. I heard about men stickin' their things inside women like they was whores."

"It's what men and women do," Rufus insisted.

She rushed at him and delivered a quick series of punches and slaps. "Not me!" she shouted. "Where's water 'round here," she demanded.

"I'll take you," he offered.

"You stay away from me. Point me the way."

Rufus pointed her toward the west. Grumbling, still bent and clutching her crotch, she disappeared.

Rufus turned to see the four members of his gang, all shaking legs and tugging at their pants. He ignored them as he stomped after Theodosia. He needed to wash his bleeding arm.

The water chattered softly as it raced across the streambed rocks. He saw her, naked in the water, scrubbing at the bloodstain on her dress. He kept his distance as he leaned to dip his arm in the cold stream. She saw him and grandiosely paid him no mind. He rinsed his arm, and then sat, penitent. The blue-gray had almost faded into night, just a hint of red about it. He watched her to the water's prattling, her naked body against the backdrop of earth and trees and sky. She was the most beautiful thing he had ever seen. Even more beautiful than the Angel of his dream because she was real and he could touch her.

As the darkness fell, she wrung out her dress and emerged shamelessly naked from the water. Rufus tentatively walked toward her. She scowled but did not protest. He stopped five feet from her and stared at his feet.

"I need somethin' to wear," she said.

His eyes brightened. He instantly dashed up toward the camp. She heard the trees and bushes rattling as he barged through them. She threw her dress over the undergrowth to dry. Again she heard the bushes thrash and Rufus reappeared with one of his shirts and a pair of trousers. Panting, he held them out toward her. With less of a scowl, she took the shirt and put it on. It fell almost to her knees. He offered the pants, but she declined. She barely glanced at him as she shouldered past and flounced back toward the camp. Rufus followed a few paces behind. As he did, four heads peeked out from behind a screen of brush.

Rufus exhaled with relief when she plopped down by his bed roll. He slowly approached and, with feigned unconcern, sat next to her, staring at the last sliver of light on the horizon. She ran her fingers through her wet hair and pulled the blanket to her chin as she lay down to sleep. As she closed her eyes, he quietly, slowly stretched himself out next to her, and lightly slipped beneath the blanket. He closed his eyes in silent thanks when he felt no resistance. Unbeknownst to him, she smiled.

~ ~ ~

With earth-rattling thunder and buckets of rain, thick, bruised skies raged at everything beneath them. In the distance, bolts of lighting slit the sky.

At first, the distant screams seemed part of it, an aural accompaniment to the hot, ominous blue-gray shroud thrown across the world. Had any man dared to walk about in the still-dark with the skies mimicking the violence awaiting every white man and woman, he would have seen figures in the distance, charging closer to Tahlequah. He would have heard the sound grow with the approaching figures. And then he would have recognized horses, their rhythmic hoofs: horses and wagon at a gallop. Then, he would have understood.

It was screaming. Atop the wagon's rattles and creaks, the horses pounding, a mindless wail, less demanding than an infant's and all the more unnerving because it seemed so rootless and unreasoning. Just a monotonous keen, meaningless enough to denote madness and constant enough to threaten the same.

The wagon approached and the screaming grew louder. It awakened the townspeople. They gazed out their windows and wondered if this is what they had so desperately feared and what they had sworn to fight. This ungodly sound, they thought, might herald the Bucks.

The most practiced hands trembled on their rifles as the

wagon raced into town, driven by an open-mouthed, bloody, wild-eyed man who screamed as if sound itself propelled him. Guns pointed at the wagon sagged as men saw the state of the driver. They thought the wagon might gallop straight through town but the horses read some undetectable slackening of will and slowed. Men surrounded them and brought the wagon to a stop. And the screaming continued. Henry Hassan sat atop the wagon, his eyes wide and staring at nothing ahead, his mouth wide and hollering, "Aaaaaaaaaaaaaaaaaaaaa," until he had no breath and sucking in air like a drowning man to do it again.

"Aaaaaaaaaaaaaaaaaaaaaaaaaaaaaaaaaaaaaaaaaaaaaa. Aaaaaaaaaaaaaaaaaaaaaaa."

The crowd puzzled. Heads shook. In the back of the wagon sat an old woman cradling weeping children and a woman lying flat on her back. The prone woman stared at nothing, straight up at the sky, silent. The children cried softly. Townswomen moved to comfort them.

A man climbed next to Henry Hassan, marveled at his butchered face, and shook him. Hassan did not stop screaming. The man shook him harder, and Hassan turned his face to him. The long, endless screams changed to shorter ones, and then to staccato bursts. Henry Hassan raised his hands, which shook like a palsied man's.

"What happened?" What happened, Henry?"

"Aaaaaaaaaaaaaaaaaaaaaaaa..." The screaming started again.

"It's okay. It's okay."

"Get the doctor."

They talked Henry back to his intermittent bursts as they

pulled him from the wagon, as his wife was carried down the street and his crying children tended.

That's how the Territories learned of the outrage at the Hassan farm.

10

The widow and her sons drove two covered wagons containing their worldly belongings as the Bucks swooped down on them. At gunpoint, the gang rifled one wagon, taking everything of value, and ordered the sons to drive it away. Reluctantly and at gunpoint, they left their mother and the other wagon with the Bucks.

The widow was forced to strip. Each one of the gang, in turn, then climbed beneath canopy alone with her. Her screams stopped after the second of them.

"She dead?" Theodosia asked Rufus as he, the last, emerged.

"Uh uh. She ain't movin' but she's breathin.'"

Theodosia raised her eyebrows smirkingly and walked away.

Rufus felt her chastisement. She had said he'd better start killing or they would kill him. He considered going back. He even took his gun from its holster, but found that he couldn't. He conjured the scene—the pleading eyes, the revolver's noisy lurch, and then the blood splatter and the stillness—all alone inside the tiny wagon. It would be like Garrett all over, but without the open sky to justify and waft away the stain. He feared that he might hear the ringing again; and that this time it might never stop.

"Killin's for men!" he shouted after Theodosia the moment he thought of it; but she paid him no mind.

~

The young white man they found between Okmulgee and Checotah had no idea that he had been condemned to die. They rode calmly upon his camp in the evening. He greeted them and asked what he could do for them. They pulled their guns and stripped him of his belongings. Rufus remained in his saddle, Theodosia seated behind him, as the others picked through and divided his few belongings. The young man looked on resignedly, assuming that having taken everything, they'd be on their way.

"I don't like him," Maoma announced. "I say we kill him."

The man's eyes widened.

"Let's vote on it," Maoma said as the man looked on, disbelieving. His mind raced so fast he couldn't conjure the words to plead for his life or convey his astonishment.

Sam's hand flew up. Maoma's followed. There was a pause as Rufus felt Theodosia's warm pressure up against him. He, too raised his hand. The moment he did, Lewis and Luckey shot their palms in the air. Once the unanimous hands had been acknowledged, arms fell slowly, and in silence.

The man had never had much and expected little more. But he, who had harmed no one in his life, who carried no gun—he had not expected to die so soon, nor to die in violence. He had a few, appropriately small plans, but as he dreamed small, he had as much hope of fulfilling his dreams as any. In the quiet, he thought of them: the man for whom he broke sod all day offered to take him on permanent. He could settle down. He wanted a horse of his own—a palomino—a type he had always admired.

The shot startled them. They jumped like colts. The man just stood there for a moment as the blood stained his shirt. Smoke seeped from Maoma's gun. His sidekick Sam quickly snapped off two more ragged shots that sent the man spinning to the ground. Sam beamed with pride.

Maoma marched to Sam and slapped him on the side of the head with his gun. "What'd you go an' do that for. I'd o' killed him."

"I was helpin'," Sam whined.

"Don't need no help shootin' a man," Maoma grumbled as he stomped to his horse.

Theodosia leaped from Rufus' saddle and walked to the bleeding figure on the ground. She fell on her knees as if to pray and looked at his face.

"His eyes is open. He ain't dead."

All ran toward the man.

"He ain't breathin'," Lewis said. "His chest ain't movin."

"Can he see us?" Luckey asked.

"I shot him. He's dead," Maoma insisted.

Rufus kicked at him once, and then again. "He mus' be dead. He ain't movin' and he's got three holes in him."

Theodosia leaned forward and touched one of his eyes. The lid slipped shut. The man now had one eye open.

"He's winkin' at me," she smiled. They all laughed. She then touched the other lid and dragged it down.

"Now he's dead," she announced. She smoothed his hair and placed his arms neatly at his sides. She took Rufus' hand as she rose.

~ ~ ~

In the next two days, four women in four towns claimed ravishment at the hands of the Rufus Buck gang. Each had a tale more harrowing than the last. Parker's Marshals were tracking the Bucks, and it was unlikely that rapes 100 miles apart were committed by the same men within 24 hours, especially when they'd recently been sighted another 50 miles from either. But hysteria had taken over, and the Bucks monopolized the mind of the Territories, simultaneously raping women in Okmulgee and Checotah, stealing horses in Muskogee that same night, and burning half the houses in between. Men torched their own barns and women clawed their own faces and ripped their own clothes to convince the world that they'd been singled out to be touched by pure evil.

Parker received a letter from Sam Brown, the Euchee Indian Chief, ensuring his full cooperation in capturing the Buck gang. The Creek Light Horse would be at Parker's disposal, the letter assured. Even here in Ft. Smith—not even part of the Territories—people talked of little else. The stories were so gruesome, the images so otherworldly that the mere human imagination could not resist them. Folks dwelt on them like newborns, imagining and embellishing, telling and re-telling, and most of all, personalizing—women seeing themselves desperately shielding their modesty in the face of gun barrels held by dark men who slavered for lust and vengeance; men fighting to the death to protect their women from the shameless fiends.

"I tell you what I'd o' done..." was the relentless introduction to a fantastic tale of wholly imagined valor.

Few on the streets talked of murder. John Garrett had been all but forgotten. Callahan's Negro farm hand had lived. They had not yet heard of the young man at the camp.

On Tuesday August 6, 1895, eight days after the killing of Marshal John Garrett, the District Attorney at Fort Smith formally charged Rufus Buck, Lewis Davis, and Luckey Davis with premeditated murder. He also charged all five gang members for "an assault on Sam Houston, a Negro and not an Indian... with intent then and there feloniously, willfully and of their malice aforethought to kill..." As evidence of the gravity of threat of their crimes, 12 of the district's 18 deputies were assigned to capture or kill the Rufus Buck gang.

As Judge Parker read the charges, Virgil Purefoy knocked lightly on his door. Entering, he wore a pained expression as immoderate as all of his others. He stood almost at attention.

"The Ayers girl," he intoned, "one of the first of Buck's victims... the one... violated as her father was watching... she's dead." Virgil hung his head to denote appropriate solicitude.

"How?" Parker asked.

"They don't know," Purefoy replied. "They found her dead in her room."

"Did she take her own life?"

Purefoy shook his head. "I don't know, but they said she'd

gotten weaker the last few days."

The girl had seemed so proud and strong. Parker had admired that in her, a true pioneer woman, adept at sloughing off the past and moving on. Her strength was the reason he had asked her to stay. He had assumed the Buck gang's quick capture, and he looked forward to her powerful testimony in court.

"She had to have died of something," Parker said peevishly.

"I'll find out, sir." Purefoy left the room.

Parker sat back in his chair, too shaken to continue his work. At first he wondered why this death pained him so. But the fact that she died in his town and under his protection ... it made a difference. Would she have lived if he had not asked her to stay? A strong woman of the Territories was a woman nonetheless. She had suffered the greatest insult any woman could, one from which most would never recover, and he had asked her to remain and idly count the days before imparting her shame to the world.

"God forgive me," he muttered.

Another knock at the door.

"Come in," he barked.

Purefoy reluctantly re-entered. "Something I forgot to add, sir."

Parker waited. "Go on."

"The last report had something new. They said that there was a girl with the Buck gang. A white girl, about twelve or thirteen years old."

"We've had no reports of a kidnapped girl."

"They said she was quiet, but didn't look scared. Said she wasn't tryin' to get away, either."

"What are you saying?"

Purefoy hemmed and hawed, as if he didn't dare suggest it. "A couple of the widow's sons made it sound like she might have been with them."

"Nonsense!" Parker spat. "What could a young girl do but remain quiet and try to stay alive." Parker turned from Purefoy. "Check the localities. See about a missing girl."

"Yes sir."

"And keep this quiet," Parker added. "Not a word to the papers or anyone. Just the Marshals."

"Yes sir."

As Purefoy left, a renewed sense of urgency shook Parker. His Marshals had to find them soon. A young girl in their midst. The public would go mad if they knew. Hysteria would overwhelm all reason.

He then considered the young girl. A strong woman had succumbed to an ordeal with the Bucks. What chance had she? He shook his head to eradicate the filthy images his own mind immediately conjured. He choked back a mouthful of bile at the thought of her helplessness and anguish. The idea of one of God's most innocent so besmirched literally sickened him.

~ ~ ~

For four days, Bill Swain had camped near the spot where the niggers took his daughter. He did little but scan the distance for her skipping figure returning, as always, from one of her private adventures. In four days she had not come. She had never stayed away for more than four hours. He played the scene over and over. How she looked at him with contempt, and walked to them, calmly climbing atop the horse. And again and again he dismissed the image, insisting that she had no choice, that she knew she had no choice. They had guns. They were outlaws. As he waited, two passing wagons had stopped to warn him.

"You better get back to town," the first driver said, "the Rufus Buck gang's maraudin' out here. They're rapin' women and killin' men."

He said nothing about his encounter. How could he? He couldn't admit that his daughter had ridden away with them. Something in him knew she had. She hadn't been scared. She had wanted to go. He sat out here waiting, beneath a blistering sun and violent storms... He had sat out here like Jesus in the desert not to receive Truths, but to deny them. The question now was how to make it good—how to shield himself, yet again, from the shame and blame that were surely his to bear. It was, it seemed, his life's work.

The old letter screamed as he concocted his tale.

> *You dragged me to the fields and hoed some rows and threw some seeds like they would come up overnight. When they did not, you spat and cursed me, as if it had been my fault. When old Remmie, the only nigger left on the place, tried to tell you how to make crops grow, you took a shovel and beat him half to death screaming that you were a white man and no nigger had anything to tell a white man.*

You sold everything for a carpetbagger's pittance. I asked you where we would go and how we would live. You never answered.

It was that man whose daughter would run away with niggers. He had spent his life running from that man. He was not that man. She had been grabbed and forcibly taken. He saw in his mind her violent struggle, her kicks and screams for her father's loving arms as the vicious black hands grabbed at her, touched her all over, lurid and leering and he, her father and protector, despite the guns pointed at him, lunged and heaved so hard to save her that three of the gang had to hold him back. He played the scene repeatedly until it stank of truth, until he could hear every cry and see every tear that ran down his lovely daughter's face. He had been wronged, his daughter brazenly abducted, her innocence stolen, her beauty probably ruined, her chastity surely profaned. He threw his belongings into his wagon and climbed aboard. He pointed his horse for Okmulgee.

There, he reported an unspeakable crime.

11

Henry Hassan, whose wife was left mute and insensate after her ordeal with the Bucks, leased a farm northeast of Orcutt. The morning the Buck Gang arrived, just as most mornings, Henry Hassan had considered himself blessed.

"What happened to you at the Hassan's?" Parker asked, resisting the urge to grab the beautiful, bedraggled girl's shoulders and shake her—to unleash the flood of tears that surely hid behind the calm façade—to free her outrage and regret. Seeing her beat her breast and tear her hair at the remembered horrors of her ravishment would purge her of the stain, purge him of his doubt about her part in this.

Theosodia flashed a smile so beatific that he instantly longed to touch her face and pay homage to the purity it signified. This was the girl—the innocent, the vision—whom the desperate Bill Swain had so tenderly described. It was the image that had moved Parker to invite the anguished father to kneel and pray beside him to almighty God for her safe return. This smiling gift was the child who inspired the father's unmistakable air of humility and supplication as he so fervently, so devotedly entreated the Lord—the girl who prompted the hardscrabble father to desperate prayer.

"Three of 'em held me," Bill Swain had wept, "and I struggled with every piece o' strength the Lord gave me, but may He in all of His mercy forgive me... it was not enough." His tears moved Parker deeply.

"Who's Hassan?" the wide-eyed object of the father's prayers now asked the Judge.

"The lady with the husband and children. On the farm."

"They had great big pigs," Theodosia giggled.

"What happened to you there?" Parker repeated. "You can tell me. You can tell me what they did to you. You're safe here."

"I am?" she asked, prompting Parker's heart to race with anticipation.

"Yes. Yes, girl. You are. Nothing like that will ever happen to you again. Your father and I will promise you. Tell me."

He had mined for suffering. Now hoped to find it. Like a ghoul, he wanted tales of savagery and defilement—any outrage to this girl's person or dignity. Parker knew that this beautiful little girl could not have tolerated the barbarities these dark fiends let loose on his Territories, that she stood as removed from raping and torturing as he—who had striven to live according to God's holy word—once believed he stood from eternal damnation. He brutally snatched at her innocence like an infant does its mother's teat; like a drowning man at a paltry scrap of wood.

"Tell me," Parker begged her.

"That other man's eyes was open;" she began as if in the middle of her tale, "but that lady... Hassan... her eyes was closed and she looked dead, but she was still breathin'. I closed the man's eyes an' they stayed shut, an' he was truly dead 'cause you can't be dead with your eyes open. So I tried holdin' her nose to stop her breathin' so she could be dead, too. But she didn't stop breathin' an' be dead like he did."

Theodosia paused to play with her fingers.

"Why wouldn't she die?" she asked with all of the innocence Parker dreamt to see in her.

~

Seeing the riders coming on, Henry Hassan paused to watch. Hassan dropped the hay he was feeding and strode toward them, a calm smile on his face, assuming they were lost, or thirsty. If so, he would offer directions and water, or have his wife fix them some food. He saw the color of their skin, counted their numbers and then he stopped. He remembered the stories he'd heard—about the horrors.

Then he saw the guns.

He turned to run, but a bullet scored the ground at his feet. He stopped and turned to face them. Five of them. Indian and colored. Five revolvers pointed at him. The Rufus Buck gang. He raised his hands.

"Henry!" He heard his wife call.

"Get the children inside and lock the door," he yelled. "Now!"

From the doorway, Rosetta Hassan saw the riders. Two of her three small children played near the house, Rosetta's elderly mother overseeing them.

"Mama, bring the kids in. Hurry up."

Her mother, frozen at the sound of the shot, looked nervously at the riders as she shooed the children toward the house. Once they'd piled in, Rosetta Hassan slammed the door and dropped the lock. She then dashed to a cabinet and pulled a revolver. She checked to make sure it was loaded.

In the quiet, she waited. One of her children wept softly and she opened her arms, cradling a weeping child with one hand, holding a revolver on the other.

Outside, the riders surrounded Henry Hassan. He recognized the mean-looking one named Maoma. A couple of months prior, Maoma had passed through Hassan's farm. Hassan had asked him to close the gates behind him—a request Maoma had belligerently refused.

"Get us some water," Rufus demanded.

Every creak of a saddle, every rumble from a pig or cry from a flying bird was like a whip crack in the stagnant silence. Hassan's pants snapped loudly as he walked to the well. The pail smashed down and the pulleys wailed as he hauled the sloshing pail back up. He lugged it to the riders, held it aloft, and let Rufus pull the ladle and drink. The scene had been so unnerving that Hassan hadn't registered the girl. Now, as she lifted the ladle and smiled sweetly at him, he jerked his head to Rufus, about to protest, but thought better of it. Rufus nodded, instructing Hassan to serve the others. Hassan did as he was bid.

When he had served the last, Rufus said, "This is a nice place," as he looked around the Hassan farm.

"I got this place fair," Hassan argued.

"Ain't no white man on Indian land got it fair," Rufus said. "We're takin' it back."

"You better get goin'," Hassan said, trying to sound helpfully conspiratorial. "They're all after you... the Marshals. They gonna catch you up soon. If you go now, you can outrun 'em.

You can leave the girl here. She won't slow you down." Hassan looked sympathetically at Theodosia.

"You gonna kill him?" she asked.

"If he don't leave," Rufus replied, "we gonna kill 'em all."

"If you do, I get to close his eyes like the other one," she said.

Hassan shook his head as if to clear it and deny what he had heard. He held his arms imploringly toward the girl.

"You come on down, honey, and we'll take care of you," he coaxed.

"You got no place to stay, no place to live," Rufus said. "How you gonna take care o' somebody?"

Hassan wiped sweat from his lip.

"Luckey, who's in the house?"

Luckey and Lewis glanced at one another, as if to snap themselves into perfect sync. They dismounted in unison and pushed on the door. Locked.

"Open it up," Luckey called.

Silence.

Luckey stood back as Lewis shot a bullet through it.

Hassan lurched as if to run, but two more bullets anchored his feet to the ground.

After another moment, they heard the latch. The door creaked open. Rosetta Hassan stood there, three small children surrounding her, and an old woman behind.

"You can take a horse and a cart," Rufus said. "Nothing else."

"Henry!" Rosetta called.

"You stole this land," Rufus added.

"You can't get nowhere," Hassan pleaded. "They all after

you. The Lighthorse. Everyone. You better run. Jus' run. We won't say nothin.'"

"'Bout now, all the Indians in this Territory is takin' their land back, getting' rid o' thieves like you. You don't walk out livin', we'll carry you out dead."

"Indians is after you, too. I told you. The Creek Lighthorse is huntin' you down. Indians want you caught just as bad as white. Everyone's after the Rufus Buck gang."

Sam looked questioningly to Maoma, who shifted nervously in his saddle.

"Let's take what we can an' go," Luckey called.

Rufus barely bothered to aim as he shot. The bullet grazed Hassan's calf. He fell, shouting at the fierce pain.

"He's bleedin,'" Theodosia announced.

Rosetta ran to her husband and held him in her arms. She reached for the wound as if a touch could heal it. She wept as she rocked him.

"Indians gonna take it all back once they hear what I done," Rufus insisted.

"It's all over the Territory," Hassan panted. "Everybody knows. They all know. They all huntin' you down. Dead or alive. You better jus' run. Run and leave us be."

Rufus leapt from his horse and charged at Hassan.

He knocked Rosetta away with the butt of his gun and grabbed the front of Hassan's shirt. "I know Cherokee Bill," he yelled in the shocked Hassan's face. "We had a plan to take it all back."

"Cherokee Bill's gonna hang," Hassan pled through trembling lips.

"But the rest of us ain't," Rufus screamed at him. "We all

comin' for ya.'"

"There ain't nobody else!" Hassan shouted, as if driven mad that his truths would not take hold. "Ain't no Indians killin' white folks but you."

No lie had ever been so vile, Rufus thought. No man so foul for telling one.

~

"He said the man was gonna pay for lyin', an' 'cept for my Daddy, I ain't never seen nobody so mad," the girl recalled to Parker. "Rufus started hittin' him real hard with his gun. He was bleedin' from all over his face. His whole face was red. Like a red Indian." She giggled at her joke.

"It must have upset you to see that. Did you want him to stop?" Parker entreated, aching for it to be true. "Didn't you beg him to stop?"

She picked up a book from the table beside her. She stopped talking and gave it her full attention, obviously enjoying the feel of the tender leather, her fingertips tracing the tiny veins running through it. She looked at Parker and smiled. She examined the gold lettering that she could barely decipher. Again she flashed her appreciation at the ailing Judge.

Parker trembled and closed his eyes as she conferred her blessings on the abominable book.

~

Flaps of raw flesh hung from Henry Hassan's face. Rufus raised his arm to bring the pistol down again, so slick with viscous blood that it flew from his hand as if purposefully flung. So Rufus used his fist.

Rosetta Hassan made another of her wavering, hysterical charges at Rufus. Again Sam struck her to the ground. She screamed and wailed like a grievously wounded animal—the only sounds, now that her husband had stopped begging for mercy. Now, barely conscious, he only swayed to the rhythm of the blows. Rufus strained every muscle to keep his victim's dead weight upright.

Theodosia slipped from the saddle and walked toward the carnage. She leaned forward, her arms out to her sides. She stuck her neck out to its fullest and opened her mouth in an expressive "O". She bent her knees so that she crouched as she oh so slowly circled the scene. Then she slowly flapped her arms like giant wings.

"Bawk," she cried. "Bawk!"

She flapped her arms in a sudden flurry, as if willing herself to ascend, and then she flapped them slowly once again. Rosetta Hassan stared at her in amazement.

"Bawk. Bawk!" Theodosia made a sudden dash at the wife, as if to peck her eyes out, and then retreated just as quickly.

Rosetta Hassan screamed. As if glimpsing the hell she feared, she screamed long and loud, so loudly that Rufus stopped beating her husband and turned to her. He released Henry Hassan and strode to the screaming wife. He grabbed her hair and dragged her toward the barn. Her screams redoubled and her hands clawed at his hands as her legs kicked at the brown, chalky dirt.

After swaying like a tree half-felled, Henry Hassan slipped to the ground.

"Come on!" Rufus ordered.

"What about them?" Lewis asked, indicating the old woman and the children.

"Bring 'em."

Having gained her knees if not her legs, Rosetta Hassan intermittently crawled and staggered as Rufus pulled her by a handful of hair. Once in the barn, he threw her to the ground.

"Take off your clothes," he ordered.

She grabbed her dress tightly around her. Maoma and Sam entered, and even Maoma did not instantly exult in this display, its outline too unpredictable, its outcome open-ended, it's violence as likely to splatter on him as anyone else. Lewis and Luckey followed, herding the old woman and the children inside the barn.

Rufus stormed toward them, grabbed one of the children and pointed a gun at his small head.

"Take 'em off or I kill him," he said.

With a new burst of tears, Rosetta Hassan slowly unbuttoned her dress. Her old mother bit her lip to fight back tears, and averted her eyes.

"Please take the children away. Please!" the old woman wept.

Rosetta asked herself what sins she had committed. As she unbuttoned her dress, exposing more and more of her flesh, a gun pointed to her young child's head, she thought back on her life to identify the acts or omissions to so anger almighty God that this should befall her. As she felt the warm air on her breasts, she admitted that she found none, that there was no sin of equal breadth for which this would be a fitting punishment. As Rufus, annoyed at the slow unveiling, ripped her dress open, she abandoned a lifetime of belief in justice, in goodness as an inviolable shield against the darkness that she knew existed in the world, but that she assumed could never touch her.

As she saw the short Negro and the tall Indian lead the children and her mother from the barn, she let go. Every muscle, every tendon relaxed, and she disappeared. She barely felt Rufus Buck spread her legs; she barely noticed his stiff member popping from his pants as he pulled them down. She stared blankly at the ceiling as he entered her and did not hear the energetic grunts or feel the pain as he violently thrust himself inside her. Nor did she hear the whelps of delight from Maoma as he urged his leader on, so distracted by the lust and violence on display that he did not notice his leader's desperation or his tears as he viciously raped Rosetta Hassan.

Outside, Lewis, Luckey, the old woman and the children all shielded their eyes from the brilliant sunlight-smeared sight of Theodosia continuing her cackling game with the prostrate Henry Hassan.

"Gawk!" she squawked as she dove in at him, her fingers snatching sharply at him like a beak before she soared off again.

The onlookers stared, rapt. Then, as if abruptly impressed with Hassan's immobility, Theodosia dropped her arms, stood straight, and stared at the bloody figure on the ground. After a period of study, she approached and hunkered down next to him. She lifted one bloody eyelid until she saw the eyeball beneath. Then she let it drop. The eye closed. She lifted it again and let it drop. Again the eye closed. She tried the other eye with the same result. She smoothed his hair and laid his arms neatly at his sides.

Satisfied, she rose and walked away. The old woman renewed her scowl of terror and disbelief as Lewis and Luckey watched the odd girl disappear into the barn. Fascinated, afraid of missing a scene of equal peculiarity to the one they'd just witnessed, Lewis and Luckey herded the reluctant old woman and the children after Theodosia—back into the barn.

With Rosetta Hassan's print dress like a full body halo on the ground around them, Sam Sampson, his pants, belt and drawers around his knees and his exposed bare backside pumping up and down, breathed heavily and closed his eyes in tight concentration as he plunged himself inside Rosetta Hassan. With his dark legs straight and close together on top of her white legs bent and spread out, they looked like a backwards/frontwards, two-toned frog. It made Theodosia giggle, breaking the lonely cadence of Sam's breathy pants.

Rufus and Maoma stood on one side of the panting man on top of the wide-eyed naked woman, her mouth half-open in what seemed an aborted expression of shock. Maoma rubbed his still-thick crotch; he had already taken her. Lewis and Luckey steered the old woman and the children into a corner, barely able to keep their eyes off the naked breasts and heaving buttocks on the ground. The old woman took in every face in the square room as if seeking confirmation that it was all really happening. She did not know what to feel. She had no emotions to apply to this; it stood outside the frame of what was human and so she could not feel it. This was more than ravishment. It was her own presence and that of the children, these men watching, her daughter's nakedness witnessed by all and her trance-like torpor amidst the repulsive violence done her. Torn between reaching out to her daughter and shielding her grandchildren from the sight—she could have held her daughter's hand as the man heaved on top of her, or cradled her head and cooed soft comforts as the naked man rutted inches away—torn between that and running away and never turning back, she stood the children in the corner with their faces to the wall, then turned her own back to the scene, conferring upon it the privacy of a rite that she could not comprehend and therefore dared not witness.

Intrigued with Rosetta Hassan's unmoving face, as still as a photograph—as still as death, Theodosia moved to the pair's heads. The breathy groans grew louder and Sam's naked thrusts more rapid and ferocious, but Rosetta's face did not change. It stared, open-mouthed and motionless, like a statue locked in prayer. Theodosia felt sad at the sight of Rosetta Hassan's face. She fell to her knees and touched it, laying her palm on the warm cheek. Rosetta Hassan did not move.

Sam moaned and uttered a short burst of grunts that rose in frequency and volume until he fairly screamed, and then fell still. He opened his eyes as if regaining consciousness, and looked at the blank white face that lay corpse-like beneath him. He shuddered as his penis slipped out of her, stood and pulled his pants up, smiling with accomplishment and satisfaction at Rufus and Maoma, the former staring glum hatred at the naked woman on the ground, while the latter grinned and nodded in camaraderie.

As Theodosia stroked the raped woman's beatific face, Luckey moved to straddle Rosetta Hassan. He unbuckled his belt, and pulled down his pants, his penis erect as he lay on her, and with one hand guided himself inside her with a sigh. Theodosia ignored Lewis as his naked backside slapped noisily against Rosetta Hassan. Enamored with the quiet beauty of the woman's deathly gaze, Theodosia placed her pointing finger on one of Rosetta Hassan's eyelids and slowly pulled it down. As she removed her finger, the lid popped open. Theodosia knew that only one thing would crown the woman's transformation to the only sublimity and purity she had known—the lifeless rigidity that lay still, sun-baked and at one with everything, as if sculpted by the earth from various elements for the big, black birds to play with, just another piece of the immobile, unspeaking nothing all over—so Theodosia tried again to close Rosetta Hassan's eyes, first one and then the other, but each time the lids popped unblinkingly open. As Luckey's rowdy grunts crescendoed and his naked backside clinched tight, Theodosia pinched Rosetta Hassan's nose. The woman's eyes continued staring fixedly toward the barn ceiling. The breathless Luckey rose to his feet while Theodosia, with one hand pinching Rosetta Hassan's nose, placed her other hand over the naked woman's mouth. All watched. Nobody moved.

Eyes still unblinkingly staring, Rosetta Hassan's stiff arms began flailing up and down against the ground as legs rhythmically kicked at straw and muffled sounds struggling for breath gurgled from beneath Theodosia's hand. The flailing hands then found Theodosia, pounding and clawing at her. Theodosia removed her hands from the woman's face to swat at the limbs now attacking her. No longer muffled through Theodosia's flesh, Rosetta Hassan's monotonal moans, like those from a slow, drooling child, grew louder.

For Theodosia, the beauty was gone. The potential to become like the stiff, dead things that so resplendently littered the land—it collapsed in that fit of graceless flapping about and mewling, so Theodosia sat on Rosetta Hassan's moaning face. She plopped her buttocks on the woman's face as if it were a pisspot. The woman's screams intermittently vibrated against her skin and dirty drawers as she giggled and bounced up and down. She went up and the screams grew louder, and down, they grew softer—louder and softer as she rose and fell. Sam laughed and Moama clapped his hands and stamped his foot in time to her bouncing and the rise and fall of Rosetta Hassan's cries.

~

Spittle flew from his lips as he held the book aloft like a preacher's Bible, red-faced and jowls trembling.

"She touched this!" he shouted at the bewildered Virgil Purefoy. "As she giggled and recounted the sickening perversions, she placed her little hand upon it as if in some vile benediction, gazed so lovingly at it—have you seen her face, beautiful, isn't it?—as close to an angel as you will ever see—and she ravished this book with her eyes as if from here she learned to hide her ugliness behind everything that civilized men find pleasing, as if from here," he said, beating on the book as if to punish it, "to cloak the bloody filth that she is, like no human creature—inhuman. She is as white as you and I with a heart as black as any on Murderer's Row. And you," he pointed at Purefoy, "you brought this here, this filth," and he heaved the book at him. "Were it not for you and this book, I never would have known... she might never have been." He ran for the book and snatched it off the ground where it lay. "As if the pages conjured her," he said. "As if to punish me for what I have done, for what I have failed to do here in this Territory. Was I so wrong? Is it," and he swept his arms as if to take in all 74,000 square miles, "is it so unforgivable that I should be punished by this land vomiting up that girl and Rufus Buck? She sat here, in all her beauty, across from me and told me laughingly of rape and degradation, of rot and death. She loves death; it enlivens her, the darkness, the stillness, the unknown, the rot and the stench that frighten ordinary men to trembling, that fills me with horror as it threatens me. She breathes it like air."

Parker fell into his chair. He rested his head in trembling hands.

After a few moments of dumbly staring at the back of Parker's head, Purefoy tiptoed toward him. He peered around the edge of the chair as if a jack-in-the-box might pop up. Instead, he saw a scared old man.

"Judge?" Purefoy whispered.

Parker slowly shook his head from side to side. "We must tell no one," he whispered.

Purefoy waited. "Not tell what?" he finally asked.

Parker rifled through phrases and pages that floated in his mind's eye like ticker tape dribbled from on high. Each shard was a piece of the prophecy, reminding him of the world The Book (and that's how he conceived it now—The Book) presaged—monstrosities born of a chaos without a Godly, guiding hand, against which all he could do was rail like a mad dog at thunder.

"We'll say what the father said, the liar—that she was forced, kidnapped, defiled by the Bucks. That's what the jury must hear. It's what the Territory will accept upon looking at her and seeing her beauty and then, across the courtroom, seeing the black faces that tortured white men and raped white women. They will weep for purity's innocence. She must represent, in its most vivid form, what these savages are capable of. Looking upon that beautiful face, they must never imagine that it is as depraved as the black ones sitting not far—perhaps more so, no righteous outrage excusing her, born with skin soft and white as cotton, born to a white man who fought for his right to reign supreme over the Rufus Bucks who now outrage their way across my Territory—behaving not as the cow-like beings we like to think them, but as viciously as we would have if similarly abased. It can't be borne. The jury will never hear of her repulsive gestures upon Rosetta Hassan. They will never conceive of the world the book foresaw. They will never know what I have made."

Purefoy was not sure what Parker meant. He assigned it to ill health and old age.

"As she parades her innocence on the stand, she will be all white men," Parker said, as if to himself. "She will be all of us."

As he rode from the Hassan farm, Rufus turned back to seal the tableau he'd left behind: Three children stood weeping as Henry Hassan dragged his bloodied, broken body, inch by inch, toward the barn where his wife lay naked and seemingly lifeless, as the old woman hysterically pulled on his arms as if engaged in absurd attempts to lift and carry him.

With Theodosia, his Angel, in the saddle behind him, Rufus felt satisfied.

12

After news of the Hassan farm, women and children traveled under armed guard. Deputy Marshals Samuel Haynes and N.B. Irwin mounted more posses to hunt the Bucks than the Territory had ever seen at one time. The Creek Lighthorse joined the hunt in numbers.

Lewis and Luckey felt it first. It was just a sense, a mild itch of finality, an inkling of chances passed, of endings.

Lewis assigned his downheartedness to Theodosia's antics preventing his full-throated enjoyment of Rosetta Hassan. He felt as if he had failed in a duty—reneged on his end of a bargain. Luckey assured him that it was no grave matter, and simultaneously wondered what accounted for his own dampened spirits.

"White folks'll think twice about comin' to the Territory after this," Rufus had announced, recalling the wreckage at the Hassan's. Lewis, though, kept hearing Henry Hassan's voice.

"There ain't nobody else," he'd said. *"Ain't no Indians killin' white folks but you."*

If that was true, Luckey thought, and they were alone, then it wouldn't be long now. The blackest of them all, not white and not even a little bit Indian, he knew he'd be the first to fall no matter who caught up to them.

"I been thinkin' about that farm," Luckey said.

"What about it?" replied Lewis.

"We oughta buy it. It's time." Lewis looked at Luckey and, as usual, they instantly understood one another.

Luckey trotted his horse up to Rufus.

"We need supplies," he said. "And some money. We oughta do some robbin'."

Rufus looked thoughtful for a moment, and then nodded his head in condescending agreement. Luckey let his horse fall back in line with Lewis.

"When we get what we want, it's time to go," he said to his friend.

"Go where? What about takin' back the Territory?" Lewis asked

"Go find a farm. Like that man said, might be nobody else. After what we done, if they catch up to us..."

As they rode in silence, each imagining himself hunted and cornered like an animal.

Rufus steered the group north, crossed the Canadian River, and held up a store in a sawmill town. Theodosia took ribbons and dresses and two little dolls. The rest stole fresh horses, cash, stocked up on guns and ammunition, and stuffed their pockets with jewelry and candy.

Exhilarated, they cantered back across the river to rob another store Maoma knew. Energized by the store's bounty and the ease with which they took it, they broke every shelf and display case as they strewed flour and sugar like New Years' revelers.

Lewis, Luckey, Sam and even Maoma were surprised when

Rufus then audaciously rode south, toward Okmulgee, which was full of law. But with their blood still up, they ignored their jitters. They galloped right over them with whoops and hollers to rob a store just West of the big town.

They bound and gagged the terrified store owner, raided the cash and stuffed meat and tobacco into gunny sacks. Theodosia was greatly disappointed when Rufus refused to linger and spread sugar and flour as they had the last time.

Word spread quickly about the string of robberies. The posses gained ground on the gang. By the time they traced the third robbery, Marshals Irwin and Hunt were no more than a few hours behind them.

Fired up by their day-long spree, Rufus stopped in a glade seven miles north of Okmulgee. He chose well. It was high ground at the base of Flat Rock, an outcropping that rose another 200 feet behind them. They could spy anyone coming from any direction.

The gang members excitedly dismounted as their horses grazed on the dry summer grass.

"Let's see it!" Maoma cried as each of them emptied pockets and dumped sacks full of everything from socks to cash into one large pile. Once pockets and bags were empty, they took a moment to appreciate the rich mound before Maoma, unable to resist, dove hungrily into it. Sam, Lewis and Luckey laughingly dove right after.

"Hold on," Rufus shouted, but the melee on the pile intensified. He pulled his gun and shot in the air.

Hunted men, they panicked at the sound of the shot, fumbling for their guns, eyes whipping in every direction to spot the vengeance that had finally found them. They awoke to their fear. It filled their throats, and they could no longer deny it, or mask its source. They had done so much—killed and raped—for the dream of awakening the Territories, but now they heard that they had failed and if the man Rufus beat half to death was right and the Territories would not awaken—then all they had done was sin like they heard about in church. Nothing more. All they could expect was retribution. Had they succeeded, had Indians risen up, their acts, however violent, would have been virtuous, like in the Good Book.

Only Rufus did not feel it. He laughed at their anxious faces, oblivious to what lurked behind them. "I'll do the dividin' here," he smiled boastfully at Theodosia, who ignored him.

As the four confirmed that the law had not found them, they slumped and sighed relief. Maoma never knew his heart could beat so fast. As they rose, the pile before them no longer gleamed like righteous bounty. It had a stain on it.

Luckey blurted, "Let's split it up an' go."

"This is a good spot," Rufus replied. "We'll camp here an' split it tomorrow."

"Let's split it now," Luckey insisted.

"What for?" Rufus asked.

"Me an' Lewis gonna buy a farm."

"Ain't enough here to buy no farm," he scoffed.

"We'll get more."

"Tomorrow. We'll camp here tonight"

"Me an' Lewis," Lucky repeated with emphasis, "gonna buy a farm."

Rufus understood. He felt dizzy. He tasted bile.

"The man said ain't no one else doin' what we doin'," Lewis

broke in, betraying little of the fear he felt.

"He was lyin,'" Rufus insisted. "That's what got him beat. He's a goddamned liar."

"We ain't seen no one," Lewis pleaded. "We ain't seen no dead white folks, no burned out farms. Ain't seen no Indians out doin' what we doin.'"

"After what we done, they're lookin' for us," Luckey explained. "If we stick together an' keep doin' the same, they gonna catch us."

It was hard to speak as he tried to staunch the spinning. "They jus' waitin' for the right time," Rufus said, his arms strangely outstretched as he tried to gain his balance. "After what we done...

"That's it," he said, as if hitting upon an irrefutable point, "after what we jus' done, they'll be comin' now. When word of them folks at that farm spreads, it'll start."

"They said the Creeks lookin' for us, too," Lewis muttered.

Rufus plopped down on the ground. He hung his head, breathing hard. The others took the novelty for rage. Inside his head, thoughts whirred and buzzed and he couldn't make sense of them. This was wrong. His success had been assured. It was predestined by an Angel of God. Providence had led him to Cherokee bill—a great man at the time—who embraced and clarified his mission. Seeing his father's pain and all those years of studying tragic mementos on shelves against the wall. These events had molded him into the man that he was, the man who could extract retribution and finally bestow justice. He had been born Indian and colored and his mother had never known her parents and his father had lost everything and he had endured S.P. Callahan calling him and his kind dirt. It had happened because God had endowed him with the strength to spill as much of the white men's blood as it took to make it right. It had been fate. This was his destiny.

~

On the prairie one mile north of where the Buck gang gathered, Marshal Samuel Haynes raised his hand and stilled his horse on hearing a gunshot in the distance. Marshal N.B Irwin and the rest of the 10-man posse, white, black and Indian, stopped behind him. Haynes turned his head in the direction from which the shot sounded. He heard nothing more. Without so much as a nod to the posse, he spurred his horse to a gallop. He knew it was them.

~

"I'm gonna go now," Theodosia sang. She skipped to the pile of loot and pulled a lace-covered doll from it. Stroking the doll's hair, without glancing at Rufus or any of the others, she sashayed confidently into the brush and disappeared.

Still reeling, Rufus thought of dreams. He looked at the puzzled faces staring at him and wondered if the last days had been that—a dream as real as the one years ago that sent shudders from his shoulders to his toes and torrents of jissom gushing from his cock. Had he killed a man... how many days... 10 days ago? He looked at the pile of takings on the ground and wondered where they'd come from. The strange scene at the Hassan farm... the beautiful Angel... All phantoms. Perhaps he'd been wounded and rode in a daze.

The world spun alarmingly.

Luckey slowly turned from him and walked toward the pile of stolen goods. Calmly, he knelt and began moving items from here to there, into piles. Lewis joined him, and then Maoma.

That's when Sam saw the dust. This, he thought, must have been what it was like for those the gang rode down upon—a dust cloud approaching, death and the devil inside.

"Folks comin'" he cried.

Rufus exhaled an audible grunt as he leapt to his feet. Flung from his mind were all the shadowy thoughts as he spied the approaching cloud. Something was coming—there was someone to fight.

"Get the ammo," he ordered as he flew to the pile and grabbed rifles and cartridge belts. Pressured by his urgency, the others did the same.

Rufus, rifle at the ready, heaved himself at the ground at the edge of the plateau. The other four threw themselves at the plateau's perimeter and their shots soon snapped like firecrackers. The posse scattered around the base of Flat Rock as the Buck gang's shots rained down. Some possemen slipped from their horses and took cover in the rocky terrain.

Rufus smiled as he fired wildly. His path once more clear, his sense of purpose restored, he felt reborn after a quick, terrifying descent into oblivion. The shots deafened him. The smoke stung his eyes. As the posse returned fire, divots exploded in the trees and ground around him.

More horses flocked to the base of the hill. Drawn by the fire, there must have been fifty men down there. Rufus whooped with excitement. This is the way the Rufus Buck Gang would go down. It would take everything the Territory had; and if the Bucks were hell bound, they'd drag enough of the Territory with them that no one would ever forget.

He glimpsed men crawling their way up the hill, sheltering behind rocks and brush. When he ran out of ammunition, he retreated to the interior to reload, and then retook his place on the perimeter.

Excitedly, he looked to his right, ready to share his exhilaration with his gang, but he saw their fear instead. He remembered that they would have abandoned him, forsworn their mission and slunk away. He was glad that this siege had forced them, against their will, to act like men.

Despite the gang's relentless fire, the possemen crept their way closer. The battle raged. By late afternoon, the Bucks had been driven to the very top of the rocks and the law, now numbering close to one hundred, crawled like ants over their original shooting ground.

Night fell and the rifle barrels shot sparks like struck matches up and down the hill. Rufus crouched in the center of the Flat Rock summit reloading when he saw Lewis and Luckey run past him. As Maoma fled in the same direction, a head broached the rim of summit and bullets scored the air all around him. The gang members shot behind them as they fled. Rufus found himself in both his gang's and the posse's lines of fire. He darted after his gang, firing blindly behind him. He almost tripped over Luckey, who rolled on the ground grasping his leg. Rufus spotted the blood trickling between Luckey's fingers, but a bullet almost singed his ear and he kept running. He glimpsed outlines of Lewis, Sam and Moama spread out before him in the thick smoke. The flaming rifles sprouted in front of them as well as behind. Rufus slid behind a tree.

He lost sight of the others. Breathless, he assumed they were dead and prepared for the same. He slipped more bullets into his revolver amidst the pepper of shots from all directions; he pumped cartridges into his rifle and then he steeled himself for one great, last run. He would go down in glory.

A deafening explosion, a blast of wind like a smack to his head ripped his guns from his hands. Dazed, smoke choked him. He couldn't breathe. He couldn't see. When he opened his eyes, at least twenty guns stared down at him.

Having grown tired of the siege, one of the possemen had shot dynamite from the barrel of his gun, bringing the gang to their knees.

~

Sickly pale with deep purple rings around her eyes, Rosetta Hassan looked like a fevered corpse as she lay in the hotel bed. Her eyes stared straight ahead although her head moved slightly in response to voices, as if to reach her, sound had to battle the barriers her trials had erected all around her.

Marshal Bass Reeves had accompanied Judge Parker to the hotel room in which she stayed under doctor's supervision, but upon seeing his black face, she began the slow, agonized keening that so frightened everyone—a sound from hell and beyond that she had learned from her ravaged husband. Reeves slipped back through the door, leaving Parker, the opulently bandaged Henry Hassan, and the doctor alone with the bedridden woman.

Parker, trembling and fighting to maintain his composure, sat in a chair next to the bed, and spoke softly.

"I hear you wish to testify against those who did this."

Her wide eyes straight ahead, as if perpetually awaiting the next terror, her head slipped toward her husband, who smiled weakly at her. She shook her head 'yes.'

"That is very brave of you," Parker reassured. He wanted to reach for her hand, but feared his tremors would be too violent and noticeable.

"We will catch them soon, I promise," he said. "They will be punished for this. You will have justice."

Her blank face did not register his soothing words.

Unable to conceive a delicate approach, he said, "The young girl..."

Rosetta Hassan's eyes flew instantly to his and a low moan grumbled in her throat. The doctor approached, took her hand and stroked it.

"It's alright now," he said. "It's alright."

The sounds fell to a labored breathing. The doctor nodded to the Judge.

"They took her," Parker said, his voice breaking. "They ripped her from her father's arms and forced upon her the same violence and degradation to which you were so brutally subjected."

Rosetta Hassan's head shifted and she stared again at the ceiling.

"Offenses barely endurable for a grown woman—imposed by men capable of lusts and evil beyond description—upon so pure a child."

A tear formed in Parker's eye. He cried for this and the surfeit of other lies he had told to the desperate.

On seeing the tear, Rosetta Hassan lifted her hand to his

face as if to touch it, but stopped halfway as if the strength or the will had left her.

Parker took her hand. There was deep pain in the exhausted old face—pain sharp enough to puncture her obsession with her own.

"Bring her," she whispered.

Parker's grip involuntarily tensed on Rosetta Hassan's hand. He released it immediately. Christian forgiveness. Rosetta Hassan would practice it. She would confer it upon the deserving innocent—as was proper. It's the sort of gesture that in his more Christian tempers, he would have made himself.

The idea of it sickened him—the depraved girl standing at her victim's bedside receiving her benediction. It sickened him; and he would endure it. He would witness it. He would assist it; and all because to do so camouflaged the world and men to the degree that he could stand to say he served a God who sanctioned them.

Parker sent his Marshal to fetch the girl's father—the filthy vagabond who recalled himself a gentleman—and for Mrs. Pinch to bring the girl. Bill Swain arrived with himself and his clothes washed—haphazardly—as if he'd lost the art of doing it properly, his skinny pants smudged and stained, his hair combed, but greasy, whether from natural oils or beautifying pomades it was impossible to tell. He worked hard to present an upright appearance, and he seemed more desperate for his efforts.

"The Buck's victim in there has asked to see your daughter," Parker informed Swain, who shook his head in grave and enthusiastic assent. "I told her that your daughter was also a victim. I asked the woman to imagine the crimes visited upon herself, but imposed on one so young." Parker searched Swain's face for the rigors of liar's remorse.

"That's jus' what happened," Swain earnestly intoned. "That's how it happened."

Parker weighed the satisfaction of calling Swain a liar against his own need to propagate the lie.

"You must see to it," Parker confided, leaning so close to Swain he could smell nervous sweat on him, "that she tells the story that you so movingly told—of abduction and rape, of desperate fear and forced participation in their filth... forced participation. It is imperative that Rosetta Hassan hears that tale," Parker leaned back to gauge whether Swain had grasped the import. "Do you understand?" Parker emphasized, intensifying his already burning gaze.

Bill Swain's simpering mien fell like a discarded costume mask. Everything about him hardened.

"I didn't do nothin' to deserve this," seethed the haggard, ill-kempt man. "I was the son o' one of the best families in Mississippi. My wife was a beauty and our children should have been the pride of the state, married to the finest, to make more of the best. That's what I was born to," he insisted, indignantly jabbing his finger at Parker as if he were to blame. "That's who I shoulda been."

Parker ignored the flared nostril outrage and focused on the disbelief—that Bill Swain could not fathom what he had become.

"And you are still that man," Parker reassured. "The jury and all the world watching this trial must see that you are. In your daughter, they must see the kind of girl that such a well-born man would raise."

"They took her," Swain exhorted as if daring one last time to convince himself. "It took three of 'em to hold me back."

Parker couldn't stand any more. Disgust overwhelmed him.

"They did not take her," he almost shouted. "She went with them because she wanted to. They did not force her." He paused to settle his temper, but instead grew more and more incensed. "She enjoyed it!" Parker hissed at him.

Angry tears filled Bill Swain's eyes.

"No one will believe the Bucks. You just make sure your daughter tells the same lies that we so deftly tell—both to that poor woman in there whom she helped terrorize, and on the witness stand."

Swain wept.

Softening, Parker added, "You cannot live with the idea of what she's done. I understand. Nor can I. The world in which she could do this... it is not the world we made. Not the one we meant to." Self-pity and guilt descended like a mist.

"We deserved better," he mumbled to himself as he turned away from Swain. "Our memories need not be stained with this."

13

As the Rufus Buck Gang was run to ground at Flat Rock summit, Cherokee Bill stood trial in Judge Parker's court for the murder of jail guard Lawrence Keating. The trial lasted three days, at the end of which Bill was found guilty and sentenced to hang. The day after his sentence, he received a visit from the man who had condemned him to die to discuss the mind and motives of young Rufus Buck.

Legal maneuvering, the details to which he'd long since stopped attending, delayed Bill's execution; so he was still in his cell when Buck returned to Ft. Smith—not for petty thievery or liquor running this time, but to the first floor—Murderer's Row.

Henry Starr had been Bill's sole source for information since his failed breakout and subsequent close confinement. Bill was not surprised to hear that Rufus had been likewise confined. If Starr was to be believed—and that was always a question—Buck's crimes had far bettered Bill's in the outlaw department. A lot of rape and murder, they said. The whole Territory terrified. Bill tended to believe it. Parker's visit had telegraphed the scare Buck had put in the white folks; and nothin' scared white folks like a rapin', killin' Negro. Bill felt a twinge of pride. He admitted to himself a certain excitement at Buck's return. Recalling the obstacles he had originally overcome to seek him out, Bill figured the boy would show up somehow—close confinement or not. 'Little Rufus Buck,' Bill thought, 'made it to the first floor.'

Rufus never came.

"How come we ain't seen nothin' o' him?" Bill asked Henry Starr after a week or so.

"They think he's worse than you," Starr said. "He ain't getting' outta that cell."

"You seen him?" Bill asked.

"No," he replied.

He had not thought of Buck. He forced himself not to. Shame was the culprit, but he did not dwell on it. He had lied to Buck and manipulated him, and then during happenings resulting from his lies and manipulations, he had saved Bill's life while simultaneously betraying him to win freedom for himself. He chuckled bitterly inside. It was typical of him—so morally immoral, so uprightly low down.

"Think he'll watch me hang?" Bill asked.

Starr shrugged. "Don't know if he'll ask. Don't know if they'd let him."

Deep down, Bill wanted him there. No one had ever looked up to him like that. He had never inspired anyone. Buck there would prove that he had meant something.

~

On March 17, 1896, the whole jail—the whole Territory—knew that Cherokee Bill would die. Rufus Buck knew, though he should have been dead. The Judge had originally set the Buck Gang's hanging for October 31, 1895. Supreme Court review then delayed their executions until July of 1896. Rufus wished that they had died before Bill. He didn't know why.

Six months had passed in solitude and stillness, despite the clamor and stink of the Ft. Smith jail. Rufus rose, he ate, he slept, armed guards walked him in the yard, and then he did it all again. He thought of little. He thought of dying and decided that the act itself did not impress him. He convinced himself, however, that his death would finally unleash the upheaval that he had worked so hard to incite in life. So he learned to anticipate death as children do Christmas. It would bring the greatest gift.

To secure his martyrdom, he took to writing letters. Addressed "To the Indian people of Indian Territory," the letters explained how their freedom had been slowly stolen, how their land had been usurped, their dignity ground to dust. Day after day he wrote, seeking new, improved and more persuasive ways to tell his tale. He wrote about the forces that compelled his quest, the Divine presence that guided him, and the Angel that came first in a dream and then in the flesh to accompany him. He told how he had sought to free all of the Indian and colored people. He prophesied that in death, he would succeed.

He waited for her. Any commotion in the jail and he sat up, hoping that she had come. He forgave her for the trial. It hurt that she had barely looked at him, but he knew in his heart that they made her say those things. It wasn't her fault.

So that Rufus could remain God's servant to his people, so that Parker could remain the righteous architect of Territories, so that Bill Swain could remain a gentleman, Theodosia remained the innocent. To Rufus, she was God's voice in his ear. So white, and so pure; she was all good things on this earth.

~

The unimaginably frail Rosetta Hassan took the stand and spoke unsteadily of her ordeal at the hands of the merciless Buck gang. She wept. During her frightful testimony, the jury glared with open hatred at the five defendants, who sat unmoved.

As Rosetta Hassan was led from the witness stand, the Judge called Theodosia Swain in trembling disbelief at his own actions, his own voice disembodied, as if as if it bled, hollow, from another world. Everything before him flickered as if projected from a distance.

Rosetta Hassan smiled adoringly and sympathetically as she passed the child, who was dressed in white and pale pink. The gallery audibly gasped at so beautiful a creature called to speak on so grisly a crime. After swearing in, Theodosia sat to give her testimony.

"Do you recognize these men here?" the prosecutor asked, pointing to the defendants.

Theodosia lowered her eyes. "Yes, sir," she replied, so softly that few in the courtroom could hear her.

"How do you know these men?"

She paused, appearing to most as if the event were too painful to recall. "They took me," she said, sneaking a peak at the jury. Seeing the men paying her rapt attention, she could not help but flash a smile in their direction, which sent them nodding and smiling at one another like proud grandfathers. She looked at the gallery audience, preparing to do the same, but caught her father's glowering face and resumed her diffident air, staring at her lap and only occasionally allowing her eyes to flutter upwards.

"What do you mean, they took you?"

"They took me from my Papa," she said, looking up at her father in the gallery.

All eyes turned to Bill Swain, who, in order to appear visibly shaken, hung his head.

"He tried to stop 'em," she continued with more vehemence. "It took three of 'em to hold him back." She beamed at her father, who returned a tremulous, tear-stained smile of his own. The courtroom was spellbound.

"What happened after they took you?" the prosecutor asked.

"They made me watch."

"Did they make you watch at the Hassan farm?"

"Yes sir," her sudden broad smile disconcerted the prosecutor. Judge Parker sat in his chair, his head erect, his eyes closed as if in desperate concentration or silent prayer, willing this girl to play her part.

"Did you see these men force themselves on Rosetta Hassan?"

"Her eyes was open, too," Theodosia said, to questioning stares. Parker's own eyes popped open and he shifted in his chair. Theodosia glanced at him. "Almost as big as yours," she said to him, giggling.

Bill Swain bounced to his feet in the gallery. Murmurs

erupted.

Parker sternly addressed the witness. "Did these men force themselves on you?" he asked.

She shook her head. "Uh uh," she replied.

Parker raised his voice. "Did they do to you what they did to Rosetta Hassan?"

"I closed the man's eyes," Theodosia boasted, this time to the jury.

"Did they violate you!?" Parker thundered.

"Girl!" Swain shouted from the gallery.

All five of the Buck gang giggled as if she'd told a private joke.

"Order!" Parker thundered.

The courtroom hushed. Parker nodded to the prosecutor.

"Did they violate you?" the prosecutor repeated.

Theodosia cast an eye at the glowering Judge and then at her irate father.

"He stuck his thing in me." She couldn't help but titter.

The courtroom gasped.

"Who?"

"Rufus Buck," she replied, her shoulders squished and her head tilted in coquettish modesty.

Rufus Buck smiled shyly back at her.

"You have no further questions?" Parker asked in the tones of an order.

"No, your Honor."

"Step down," Parker said to the girl.

Her father rose. As she passed into the gallery, he grabbed her hand and marched the beautiful, smiling creature from the courtroom as she craned her neck to eye Rufus Buck one last time. Buck stood, confusing the courtroom as he gazed devotedly after her.

14

Every day, a letter arrived from the jail. Another of Rufus Buck's missives haranguing the Indians to follow his Divine lead and rise up against the white men who slowly stole their lands and their souls. Parker would have paid money never to see one of those letters again, but he trusted no one else to do what must be done—to burn each and every one of them to ashes.

His health had turned. He suffered frequent fevers. Breathing grew more difficult. Pain up and down his back nearly crippled him. It was March, and he would be officially stripped of his power in September, his court disbanded. In two days, Cherokee Bill would die. Strangely, Parker found himself moved by the latter far more than the former.

Again he visited Bill. Again his visit disordered the jail and caused widespread comment, but the dying Judge did not care.

"Have you prepared for what's to come?" Parker asked.

Bill shrugged. "You?" he asked.

"What do you mean?"

"You don't look so good."

"No," Parker sighed. "Not so good."

A silence fell that neither sought to break. Each felt quite comfortable in it. Each was part of the other's world—law and outlaw, creatures of the honest wild. They shared that.

"Do you have any requests? Any goods or messages that I can pass along?" asked Parker.

"Nah. Stole a helluva lotta money an' ain't got nothin.'"

"I've got a feeling that for you, it wasn't about the money."

Bill smiled a charming smile. "If you are right about that, Judge, I am a bigger fool than I thought."

They enjoyed another silence. Hearing nothing for so long, the guard looked in to see the Judge and the outlaw seated in phlegmatic ease.

Parker had no idea how long he'd been there when the guard's loud throat-clearing roused him.

"I'd best be going," Parker said. But he did not rise. Only when he heard the key in the lock and the creaky door swing open did he do so.

"See you soon, Judge."

"I fear so, son," Parker replied.

"Hell awaits," said Bill.

It was a struggling mass of humanity that had gathered on and around the steps and walls and when the time came there was a scramble even among those who were provided with passes. There was a crush and a jam for a few minutes but order was at last restored in a measure and all awaited the moment when the door should open for the coming of the condemned man.

The crowd outside had swelled to increased numbers, all the available buildings and sheds being occupied. A pathway was cleared through the crowd, and very shortly after the clock struck two the door opened and the doomed man was brought forth, a guard on either side. The march to the gallows was taken up.

"This is about as good a day to die as any," remarked Cherokee as he glanced around.

The death warrant was then read, during which Bill gazed about as if a little impatient to have the thing over with.

The priest offered a short prayer, the condemned man listening attentively the meanwhile, and then as if knowing what was to come next, Cherokee bill walked forward till he stood upon the trap. His arms and legs were bound, and it was while this was being done that Bill spoke to different ones in the crowd below.

> *"Good-bye, all you chums down that way," said he, with a smile. There was a creaking sound as the trap was sprung and the body shot downward. The fall was scarcely six feet, but the rope had been adjusted carefully and the neck was broken. The muscles twisted once or twice, but that was all.*

Judge Parker sat in his office during the hanging. He heard the trap door swing.

~

As his execution date approached, Rufus wrote more frantically, filling piles of paper with his scrawling mix of print and cursive, painstakingly wrought. Each day, he took desperately to his pen to redeem his cause and ennoble himself in his father's eyes.

Each day Parker received and read the writings, and each day he burned them in his fireplace. He considered it a form of private conversation—an obscene intimacy between himself and Rufus Buck.

One week before the execution, the letters stopped. On the first letter-less day, Parker told Purefoy to discover why. Purefoy reported that Rufus had written nothing that day. As subsequent days passed with no further words from Buck, Parker found that he missed them. They were the only truthful conversation he had left.

After two weeks, convinced that Buck's pen had spent itself, Parker, visibly weakening, pulled The Book from his lower desk drawer. He rose and walked to the fire and threw it on top. He then sent for Virgil Purefoy and all the court records of the Rufus Buck gang trial and sentencing.

Purefoy arrived and immediately saw the leather-bound book on the fire, the gold lettering still visible on the not-yet-blackened spine "... Species arles Darw." He said nothing as he dropped the records on the table. Parker sat down before them and gestured for Purefoy to do the same.

"It is not enough," Parker said to the confused clerk. "She must be purged." He had burned the book; and now he would erase the girl and all the connections between it and him. As if fearing it might rise from the grave, he would further bury The Book and the world it said that he had helped create.

He was half mad with the irony: the last bulwark against a Godlessly anarchic world that threatened to engulf them all; the unwitting architect of that world's monstrosities.

"We must go through these," Parker declared, flicking a hand at the records as if shooing them, "and remove all mention of her."

Purefoy protested. "Sir, these are official court records..."

"The father cannot be trusted," Parker continued. "Of course, the girl cannot. Others might be told or come to suspect. There can be nothing left."

"You look tired, sir. Why don't I..."

"Don't patronize me, boy" Parker spat, slamming his palm on the table. "You are full of idolatrous gazes and deferent sounds, but you brought filth into my house and stuck my face in it like I was some ill-trained dog. Well now you can help me clean up the mess"

"The gift was a sign of my esteem..."

"Don't you dare lecture me about the sanctity of the Court,"

Parker interrupted. "I am the court. I have been the court for 20 years. What are you?"

Purefoy visibly trembled. "I just meant, sir..."

"I'm not tired, you fool. I'm dying. Now do as I say." Parker shoved a file toward him.

They worked through the night. By morning, they had replaced the offending documents. They watched the originals burn in the fireplace, filling the room with noxious smoke. Purefoy worked in utter dismay at his and Parker's actions. No thieving or larceny would have pained him more.

When the task was done, Purefoy rose to leave.

"Take your things and go home," Parker said to him. "Back to Virginia. Go home. There's nothing left here."

"But sir, my career is here."

Parker smiled. "So you still want one, even after this? The taste is not so sour that you abandon the whole scheme?" Parker waved his hand before his face as if shooing a fly. "Stay then. You belong now. The lies that gird this place are of your making as well as mine."

Purefoy turned to go, nerve endings tingling with equal parts mortification and relief.

Holding the arm of Marshal Bass Reeves, Judge Parker attended the execution of Rufus Buck and his gang. He had to admit that they comported themselves like men. They walked calmly to the gallows. They did not weep or call out when the black hoods were placed on their heads. They ignored the taunts of the crowd.

Parker tried to resist, he tried to ignore the impulse like a drunk the bottle, but he finally scanned the crowd for the man whose pain had been so palpable that it had set this hell in motion—a pain that to this day he dreaded remembering, much less revisiting, a pain that could only have grown even more unendurable; but he did not spy John Buck among those who'd come to watch the hanging. At that—this paltry sign of God's grudging, diminutive grace—he took solace.

> *The trap dropped with its horrible "chug" at 1:25 o'clock. Lewis Davis died in three minutes, his neck broken. The necks of Sam Sampson and Maoma July were also broken, and they died quickly.*
>
> *Rufus Buck and Luckey Davis were strangled to death. Luckey's body drew up several times before it straightened out. Rufus Buck did not suffer, of course, unconsciousness coming over him as soon as the rope shut off his breath; but it was several minutes before the contortions of his body ceased.*

As the black hood fell and snuffed out the world, he writhed at the end of the rope. He gasped for air in exultation at the glorious Indian awakening his death would ignite. He would witness it, he knew, from his seat in Heaven, his Angel at his side.

As Rufus Buck hung at the end of a rope, a guard discovered a photograph in his cell. It was his mother's likeness. On the back, there was a poem in his own hand, lovingly decorated with drawings of a crucifix, ivy, and the face of Jesus Christ:

mY dreAm

I, dremP't I was in Heaven,
Among, The AngeLs, Fair;
I'd, near seen none so HAndSome
THAT, Twine in golden, Hair;
They Looked, so neat, and Sang So Sweet
And, PLAY,d, THE THE golden HArP,
I WAS ABouT To, Pick, an, AngeL ouT,
And, TAKe Her TO, mY HearT;
BuT, The moment I, BegAn, To, PLEA,
I, THougHT of You, mY LOVe,
There, WAS none I'd, seen So BeauTiFull,
On earth, or, HeAven Above.

gooDby

1Day of July
The yeore off
1896

FaATHER, Son, HOLy GHOST

virtue & resurresurrection

Judge Parker lay bedridden and desperately ill as his Court was dissolved on September 1, 1896. As the dissolution occurred, all hailed the unshakable virtue of the man who had singlehandedly civilized a once-savage land.

END

Made in the USA
Lexington, KY
09 March 2013